Some Merry Adventures
of
Robin Hood

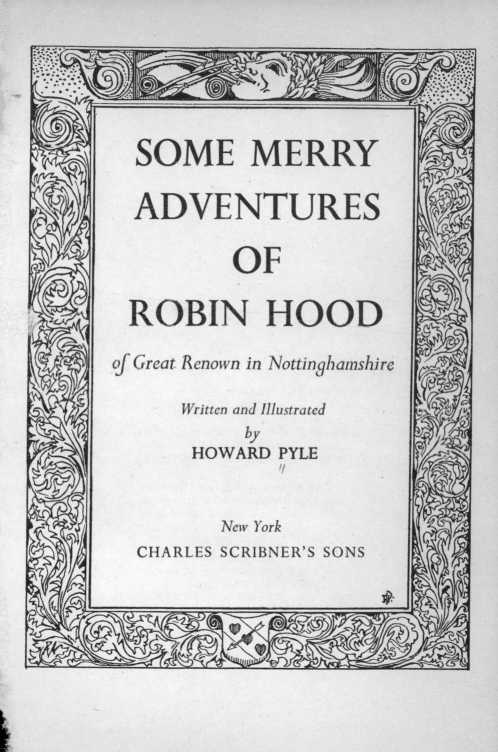

SOME MERRY ADVENTURES OF ROBIN HOOD

of Great Renown in Nottinghamshire

Written and Illustrated
by
HOWARD PYLE

New York
CHARLES SCRIBNER'S SONS

Contents

Contents

INTRODUCTION

Howard Pyle was one of America's finest illustrators. At first he made pictures for books written by other people—then he began to write and illustrate his own. All of his books show the most careful workmanship. He never wrote about or pictured any place or period without studying it carefully. As he worked on the stories they became part of himself and of his everyday life.

The legends of Robin Hood and King Arthur had indeed been a part of his life since he was a small boy. In the big house in Wilmington, Delaware, his mother read aloud to him from many books, including Malory's *Morte d'Arthur* and Ritson's collection of ballads about Robin Hood. Robin Hood, one of the earliest and best loved characters in English literature (mentioned in print as early as 1360), made a great appeal to the boy's imagination.

So, when Howard Pyle began to make his own books of heroic tales, it was natural for him to rewrite and illustrate the stories about Robin Hood. The woods around his summer studio at Chadds Ford are said to have given him much of the inspiration for the writing and pictures in *The Merry Adventures of Robin Hood*.

This small book, *Some Merry Adventures of Robin Hood,* is made up of stories selected by Howard Pyle from the larger book. It has been very popular as an introduction to a fine adventure story, and is here presented in a new edition, redesigned, reset, with pictures made from the original drawings, which are still in existence.

Boys and girls who enjoy this brief excursion into Sherwood Forest will want to read more about Robin and his band—for here is adventure, pageantry—and laughter.

Some Merry Adventures
of
Robin Hood

Yovng·Robin·goes·to the·Shooting-Match:

CHAPTER I

How Robin Hood became an outlaw and how he met with Little John

IN MERRY ENGLAND in the time of old, when good King Henry the Second ruled the land, there lived within the green glades of Sherwood Forest, near Nottingham Town, a famous outlaw whose name was Robin Hood. No archer ever lived that could speed a gray goose

shaft with such skill and cunning as his, nor were there
ever such yeomen as the seven-score merry men that
roamed with him through the greenwood shades.
Right merrily they dwelt within the depths of Sherwood Forest, suffering neither care nor want, but
passing the time in merry games of archery or bouts of
cudgel play, living upon the King's venison, washed
down with draughts from crystal fountains.

Not only Robin himself but all the band were outlaws and dwelt apart from other men, yet they were
beloved by the country people round about, for no
one ever came to jolly Robin for help in time of need
and went away again with an empty fist.

And now I will tell how it first came about that
Robin Hood fell afoul of the law.

When Robin was a youth of eighteen, stout of
sinew and bold of heart, the Sheriff of Nottingham
proclaimed a shooting-match and offered a prize of
forty marks to whomsoever should shoot the best shaft
in Nottinghamshire. "Now," quoth Robin, "will I go
too, for fain would I draw a string for the bright eyes

of my lass, for so goodly a prize as that." So up he got
and took his good stout yew bow and a score or more
of broad cloth-yard arrows, and started off from Locksley Town through Sherwood Forest to Nottingham.

As he walked along with a brisk step and a merry
whistle, he came suddenly upon some foresters seated
beneath a great oak tree; fifteen in all, making themselves merry around a huge pasty. Each man was clad
in Lincoln green, and a fine show they made, seated
upon the sward beneath that fair, spreading tree. Then
one of them, with his mouth full, called out to Robin,—

"Hulloa, where goest thou, little lad, with thy one
penny bow and thy farthing shafts?"

Then Robin grew angry, for he was mightily proud
of his skill at archery.

"Now," quoth he, "my bow and eke mine arrows
are as good as thine; and I'll hold the best of you
twenty marks that I hit the clout at three-score rods."

At this all laughed aloud, whereat Robin grew right
mad. "Hark ye," said he; "yonder, at the glade's end,
I see a herd of deer, even more than threescore rods

distant. I'll hold you twenty marks that I cause the best hart among them to die."

"Then I will take thy wager," cried one of the foresters, "and will hold thee twenty marks that thou causest no hart to die." Robin took his good yew bow in his hand, and drew the gray goosefeather to his ear; the next moment the bowstring rang and the arrow sped down the glade. High leaped the noblest hart of all the herd, only to fall dead, reddening the green path with his heart's blood.

"Ha!" cried Robin, "how likest thou that shot, good fellow?"

Then all the foresters were filled with rage, and he who had wagered the twenty marks was more angry than all. "Get thee gone, straightway," cried he, "or, by all the saints of heaven, I'll baste thy sides until thou wilt ne'er be able to walk again. Thou hast killed the King's deer, and, by the laws of our gracious lord and sovereign, King Harry, thine ears should be shaven close to thy head."

Never a word said Robin Hood, but he looked at

the foresters with a grim face; then, turning on his heel, strode away from them down the forest glade. But his heart was bitterly angry, for his blood was hot and youthful and prone to boil.

Now, well would it have been for him who had wagered had he left Robin Hood alone; but his anger was hot. Of a sudden, and without any warning, he sprang to his feet, seized upon his bow and fitting to it a shaft, sent the arrow whistling after Robin.

It was well for Robin Hood that that same forester's fingers slipped the string a little, or else he would never have taken another step; as it was, the arrow whistled within three inches of his head. Then he turned around and quickly drew his own bow, and sent an arrow back in return.

"Ye said I was no archer," cried he aloud, "but say so now again!"

The shaft flew straight; the forester fell forward with a cry, and lay on his face upon the ground, his arrows rattling about him from out of his quiver, the gray goose shaft wet with his heart's blood. Then, before the others could gather their wits about them, Robin Hood was gone into the depths of the greenwood. Some started after him, but not with much heart, for each feared to suffer the death of his fellow; so presently they all came and lifted the dead man up and bore him away to Nottingham Town.

So Robin Hood became outlawed and so he came to dwell in the greenwood that was to be his home for many a year to come. Two hundred pounds were set upon his head as a reward for whoever would bring him to the court of justice.

But Robin Hood lay hidden in Sherwood Forest for one year, and in that time there gathered around him many others like himself, outlawed for this cause and for that.

So, in all that year, fivescore or more good stout yeomen joined themselves to him, and chose him to be their leader and chief. Then they vowed that even as they themselves had been despoiled they would despoil their oppressors, whether baron, abbot, knight or squire, and that from each they would take that

which had been wrung from the poor by unjust taxes,
or land rents, or in wrongful fines; but to the poor
folk they would give a helping hand in need and trouble, and would return to them that which had been
unjustly taken from them. Besides this, they swore
never to harm a child nor to wrong a woman, be she
maid, wife, or widow; so that, after a while, when the
people began to find that no harm was meant to them,
but that money or food came in time of want to many
a poor family, they came to praise Robin and his merry
men, and to tell many tales of him and of his doings in
Sherwood Forest, for they felt him to be one of
themselves.

Up rose Robin Hood one merry morn when all the
birds were singing blithely among the leaves. "For
fourteen days," said he, "we have seen no sport, so
now I will go abroad to seek adventures forthwith.
But tarry ye, my merry men, all, here in the greenwood; only see that ye mind well my call. Three
blasts upon the bugle horn I will blow in my hour

of need; then come quickly, for I shall want your aid.''

So saying, he strode away through the leafy forest glades until he had come to the verge of Sherwood. There he wandered for a long time, through highway and byway, through dingly dell and forest skirts. At last he took a bypath that dipped toward a broad, pebbly stream spanned by a narrow bridge made of a log of wood. As he drew nigh this bridge he saw a tall stranger coming from the other side. Thereupon Robin quickened his pace, as did the stranger likewise; each thinking to cross first.

"Now stand thou back," quoth Robin, "and let the better man cross first."

"Nay," answered the stranger, "then stand back thine own self, for the better man I wot, am I."

"That shall we presently see," quoth Robin, "meantime bide thou here a little while till I come again." So saying he stepped quickly to the coverside and cut a good staff of ground oak, straight, without flaw, and six feet in length. "Lo, here is a good staff,

Robin Hood · meeteth · the · tall
Stranger · on · the · Bridge

lusty and tough,'' quoth he. ''Now we will fight until
one or the other of us tumble into the stream by dint
of blows.''

''Marry, that meeteth my whole heart!'' cried the
stranger, twirling his staff above his head, betwixt his
fingers and thumb, until it whistled again.

Then followed a great and mighty battle betwixt
these two stout yeomen. Never did the Knights of
Arthur's Round Table meet in a stouter fight than did
these two. Each stood in his place, neither moving a
finger's breadth back, for one good hour, and many
blows were given and received by each in that time,
till here and there were sore bones and bumps, yet
neither thought of crying ''Enough,'' or seemed likely
to fall from off the bridge. At last Robin gave the
stranger a blow upon the ribs that made his jacket
smoke like a damp straw thatch in the sun. So shrewd
was the stroke that the stranger came within a hair's
breadth of falling off the bridge; but he regained himself right quickly, and, by a dexterous blow, gave
Robin a crack on the crown so fairly that he fell heels

over head into the water, as the queen pin falls in a game of bowls.

"And where art thou now, good lad?" shouted the stranger, roaring with laughter.

"Oh, in the flood and floating adown with the tide," cried Robin; nor could he forbear laughing himself at his sorry plight. Then, gaining his feet, he waded to the bank, the little fish speeding hither and thither, all frightened at his splashing.

"Give me thy hand," cried he, when he had reached the bank, "I must needs own thou art a brave and a sturdy soul, and, withal, a good stout stroke with the cudgels. By this and by that, my head hummeth like to a hive of bees on a hot June day."

Then he clapped his horn to his lips, and winded a blast that went echoing sweetly down the forest paths. Soon the distant twigs and branches rustled with the coming of men, and suddenly a score or two of good stout yeomen, all clad in Lincoln green, burst from out the covert, with merry Will Stutely at their head.

"Good master," cried Will, "how is this? Truly

thou art all wet from head to foot, and that to the very skin.''

''Why, marry,'' answered jolly Robin ''yon stout fellow hath tumbled me neck and crop into the water, and hath given me a drubbing besides.''

''Then shall he not go without a ducking and eke a drubbing himself!'' cried Will Stutely. ''Have at him, lads!''

''Nay, forbear!'' cried Robin; ''he is a right good man and true, and no harm shall befall him. Now hark ye, good youth, wilt thou stay with me and be one of my band? Three suits of Lincoln green shalt thou have each year, besides forty marks in fee, and share with us whatsoever good shall befall us. Thou shalt eat sweet venison and quaff from crystal springs, and mine own good right-hand man shalt thou be for never did I see such a cudgel-player in all my life before. Speak! wilt thou be one of my good merry men?''

''Ay, that will I,'' answered the other joyfully, ''for well I love the greenwood glade and well I love stout sport with such as thou, good master.''

"Then I have gained a right good man this day,"
quoth jolly Robin. "But tell me, what name goest
thou by, good fellow?"

"Men call me John Little whence I came," answered the stranger.

Then Will Stutely, who loved a good jest, spoke up.
"Nay, fair little stranger," said he "I like not thy
name and fain would I have it otherwise. Little art
thou indeed, and small of bone and sinew, therefore
shalt thou be christened Little John, and I will be thy
godfather."

Then Robin Hood and all his band laughed aloud.

"So be it, good friend," said Robin Hood. "Little
John shalt thou be called henceforth, and Little John
shall it be. So come, my merry men, and we will go
and prepare a christening feast for this fair infant."

So turning their backs upon the stream, they plunged
into the forest once more, through which they traced
their steps till they reached the spot where they dwelt
in the depths of the woodland. There had they built
huts of bark and branches of trees, and made couches

of sweet rushes spread over with skins of fallow deer. Here stood a great oak-tree with branches spreading broadly around, beneath which was a seat of green moss where Robin Hood was wont to sit at feast and at merry-making with his stout men about him. Here they found the rest of the band, some of whom had come in with a brace of fat does. Then they built great fires, and after the feast was ready they all sat down, but Robin Hood placed Little John at his right hand, for he was henceforth to be the second in the band.

Thus it was that Robin Hood became outlawed; thus a band of merry companions gathered about him, and thus he gained his righthand man, Little John. And now I will tell how the Sheriff of Nottingham sought to take Robin Hood, and how he failed therein.

The·Sheriff·of·*Nottingham*·plotting·against·Robin·sends·a·messinger·to·*Lincoln*:·

CHAPTER II

The Shooting-Match
at Nottingham Town

Now it was told before how two hundred pounds were set upon Robin Hood's head. It is now to be told how the Sheriff of Nottingham swore that he himself would bring Robin Hood to justice, and for two reasons: first, because he wanted the two hundred pounds, and next, because the forester that Robin Hood had killed was of kin to him.

But the Sheriff knew what a force Robin had about him in Sherwood, and that he could not serve a warrant for his arrest as he could upon another man that had broken the laws; therefore he was compelled to

devise some cunning trick wherewith to entrap bold
Robin.

Thus thinking the Sheriff said to himself, "This
Robin Hood hath a daring soul. If I could but per-
suade him nigh to Nottingham Town so that I could
lay hand upon him, he would never get away again."
Then it came to him that were he to proclaim a great
shooting-match and offer some grand prize, Robin
Hood might be overpersuaded by his spirit to come to
the butts. Accordingly he sent messengers north and
south, and east and west, to proclaim through town,
hamlet, and countryside, this grand shooting-match,
and everyone was bidden who could draw a long bow,
and the prize was to be an arrow of pure beaten gold.

When Robin Hood first heard the news of this he
was in Lincoln Town, and hastening back to Sherwood
Forest he soon called all his merry men about him and
spoke to them thus:—

"Now hearken, my merry men all, to the news that
I have brought from Lincoln Town to-day. Our friend
the Sheriff of Nottingham hath proclaimed a shooting-

match, and hath sent messengers to tell of it through all the countryside and the prize is to be a bright, golden arrow. Now I fain would have one of us win it, both because of the fairness of the prize and because our sweet friend the Sheriff hath offered it. So we will take our bows and shafts and go there to shoot, for I know right well that merriment will be a-going. Some of you shall clothe yourselves as curtal friars, and some as rustic peasants, and some as tinkers, or as beggars, but see that each man taketh a good bow or broadsword, in case need should arise. As for myself, I will shoot for this same golden arrow, and should I win it, we will hang it to the branches of our good greenwood tree for the joy of all the band. How like you the plan, my merry men all?''

Then ''Good! Good!'' cried all the band right heartily.

A fair sight was Nottingham Town on the day of the shooting-match. All along upon the green meadow beneath the town wall stretched a row of benches, one above the other, whereon sat knight and lady, squire and dame, and rich burghers and their wives. At the end of the range, near the target, was a raised seat bedecked with ribbons and scarfs and garlands of flowers, where sat the Sheriff of Nottingham and his dame. The range was two-score paces broad. At one end stood the target; at the other a tent of striped canvas, from the pole of which fluttered many-colored flags and streamers.

Then the herald stood forth and loudly proclaimed the rules of the game as follows:—

"Shoot each man from yon mark, which is seven-score yards and ten from the target. One arrow shooteth each man first, and from all the archers shall the ten that shoot the fairest shafts be chosen for to shoot again. Two arrows shooteth each man of these ten, then shall the three that shoot the fairest shafts be chosen for to shoot again. Three arrows shooteth each man of those three, and to him that shooteth the fairest shafts shall the prize be given."

Then the Sheriff leaned forward, looking keenly

among the press of archers to find whether Robin
Hood was amongst them; but no one was there clad in
Lincoln green, such as was worn by Robin and his
band. "Nevertheless," said the Sheriff to himself, "he
may still be there, and I miss him among the crowd of
other men. But let me see when but ten men shoot,
for I wot he will be among the ten, or I know him
not."

And now the archers shot, each man in turn, and
the good folk never saw such archery as was done that
day. Six arrows were within the clout, four within the
black, and only two smote the outer ring; so that
when the last arrow sped and struck the target, all the
people shouted aloud, for it was noble shooting.

And now but ten men were left of all those that had
shot before, and of these ten, six were famous throughout the land, and most of the folk gathered there knew
them. These six men were Gilbert o' the Red Cap,
Adam o' the Dell, Diccon Cruikshank, William o'
Leslie, Hubert o' Cloud, and Swithin o' Hertford.
Two others were yeomen of merry Yorkshire, another

was a tall stranger in blue, who said he came from
London Town, and the last was a tattered stranger in
scarlet, who wore a patch over one eye.

"Now," quoth the Sheriff to a man-at-arms who
stood near him, "seest thou Robin Hood amongst
those ten?"

"Nay, that do I not, your worship," answered the
man. "Six of them I know right well. Of those Yorkshire yeomen, one is too tall and the other too short,
for that bold knave. Robin's beard is as yellow as gold,
while yon tattered beggar in scarlet hath a beard of
brown, besides being blind of one eye. As for the
stranger in blue, Robin's shoulders, I ween, are three
inches broader than his."

"Then," quoth the Sheriff, smiting his thigh
angrily, "yon knave is a coward as well as a rogue, and
dares not show his face among good men and true."

Then, after they had rested a short time, those ten
stout men stepped forth to shoot again. Each man shot
two arrows, and as they shot, not a word was spoken,
but all the crowd watched with scarce a breath of

sound; but when the last had shot his arrow, another great shout arose, while many cast their caps aloft for joy of such marvellous shooting.

And now but three men were left of all those that had shot before. One was Gill o' the Red Cap, one the tattered stranger in scarlet, and one Adam o' the Dell of Tamworth Town. Then all the people called aloud, some crying, "Ho for Gilbert o' the Red Cap!" and some, "Hey for stout Adam o' Tamworth!" but not a single man in the crowd called upon the stranger in scarlet.

"Now, shoot thou well, Gilbert," cried the Sheriff, "and if thine be the best shaft, fivescore broad silver pennies will I give to thee besides the prize."

"Truly I will do my best," quoth Gilbert, right sturdily. "A man cannot do aught but his best, but that will I strive to do this day." So saying, he drew forth a fair smooth arrow with a broad feather and fitted it deftly to the string, then drawing his bow with care he sped the shaft. Straight flew the arrow and lit fairly in the clout, a finger breadth from the centre.

"A Gilbert, a Gilbert!" shouted all the crowd; and, "Now, by my faith," cried the Sheriff, smiting his hands together, "that is a shrewd shot."

Then the tattered stranger stepped forth, and all the people laughed as they saw a yellow patch that showed beneath his arm when he raised his elbow to shoot, and also to see him aim with but one eye. He drew the good yew bow quickly, and quickly loosed a shaft; so short was the time that no man could draw a breath betwixt the drawing and the shooting; yet his arrow lodged nearer the centre than the other by twice the length of a barley-corn.

"Now by all the saints in Paradise!" cried the Sheriff, "that is a lovely shaft in very truth!"

Then Adam o' the Dell shot, carefully and cautiously, and his arrow lodged close beside the stranger's. Then after a short space they all three shot again, and once more each arrow lodged within the clout, but this time Adam o' the Dell's was the farthest from the centre, and again the tattered stranger's shot was the best. Then, after another time of rest, they all shot for the third time. This time Gilbert took great heed to his aim, keenly measuring the distance and shooting with shrewdest care. Straight flew the arrow, and all shouted till the very flags that waved in the breeze shook with the sound, and the rooks and daws flew clamoring about the roofs of the old gray tower, for the shaft had lodged close beside the spot that marked the very centre.

"Well done, Gilbert!" cried the Sheriff, right joyously. "Fain am I to believe the prize is thine, and right fairly won. Now, thou ragged knave, let me see thee shoot a better shaft than that."

Naught spake the stranger but took his place, while all was hushed, and no one spoke or even seemed to breathe, so great was the silence for wonder what he would do. Meanwhile, also quite still stood the stranger holding his bow in his hand, while one could count five; then he drew his trusty yew, holding it drawn but a moment, then loosed the string. Straight flew the arrow, and so true that it smote a gray goose feather from off Gilbert's shaft, which fell fluttering through the sunlit air as the stranger's arrow lodged close beside his of the red cap, and in the very centre. No one spoke a word for a while and no one shouted, but each man looked into his neighbor's face amazedly.

"Nay," quoth old Adam o' the Dell presently, drawing a long breath and shaking his head as he spoke, "twoscore years and more have I shot shaft, and maybe not all times bad, but I shoot no more this day, for no man can match with yon stranger, whosoe'er he may be." Then he thrust his shaft into his quiver, rattling, and unstrung his bow without another word.

Then the Sheriff came down from his dais and drew near, in all his silks and velvets, to where the tattered stranger stood leaning upon his stout bow, whilst the good folk crowded around to see the man who shot so wondrously well. "Here, good fellow," quoth the Sheriff, "take thou the prize, and well and fairly hast thou won it, I trow. What may be thy name, and whence comest thou?"

"Men do call me Jock o' Teviotdale, and thence am I come," said the stranger.

"Then, by Our Lady, Jock, thou art the fairest archer that e'er mine eyes beheld, and if thou wilt join my service I will clothe thee with a better coat than that thou hast upon thy back; thou shalt eat and drink of the best, and at every Christmas-tide fourscore marks shall be thy wage. I trow thou drawest better bow than that same coward knave, Robin Hood, that dared not show his face here this day. Say, good fellow, wilt thou join my service?"

"Nay, that will I not," quoth the stranger, roughly. "I will be mine own, and no man in all merry England shall be my master."

"Then get thee gone, and a murrain seize thee!" cried the Sheriff, and his voice trembled with anger. "And by my faith and troth I have a good part of a mind to have thee beaten for thine insolence!" Then he turned upon his heel and strode away.

It was a right motley company that gathered about the noble greenwood tree in Sherwood's depths that same day. A score and more of barefoot friars were

there, and some that looked like tinkers, and some
that seemed to be sturdy beggars and rustic hinds; and
seated upon a mossy couch was one all clad in tattered
scarlet, with a patch over one eye; and in his hand he
held the golden arrow that was the prize of the great
shooting-match. Then, amidst a noise of talking and
laughter, he took the patch from off his eye and
stripped away the scarlet rags from off his body and
showed himself all clothed in fair Lincoln green, and
quoth he: "Easy come these things away, but walnut
stain cometh not so speedily from yellow hair." Then
all laughed louder than before for it was Robin Hood
himself that had won the prize from the Sheriff's very
hands.

"By my troth," said the Sheriff, as he sat at meat in
the great hall of his house at Nottingham Town, "I
did reckon full roundly that that knave, Robin Hood,
would be at the game today. I did not think that he
was such a coward. But who could that saucy knave be
who answered me to my beard so bravely?"

Then, even as he finished speaking, something fell

rattling among the dishes on the table, while those that sat near started up wondering what it might be. After a while one of the men-at-arms gathered courage enough to pick it up and bring it to the Sheriff. Then everyone saw that it was a blunted gray goose shaft, with a fine scroll, about the thickness of a goose quill, tied near to its head. The Sheriff opened the scroll and glanced at it, while the veins upon his forehead swelled and his cheeks grew ruddy with rage as he read, for this was what he saw:—

> *"Now Heaven bless thy grace this day,*
> *Say all in sweet Sherwood,*
> *For thou didst give the prize away*
> *To merry Robin Hood."*

"Whence came this?" cried the Sheriff in a mighty voice.

"Even through the window, your worship," quoth the man who had handed the shaft to him.

CHAPTER III

How Will Stutely
was rescued

Now when the Sheriff found that he could not overcome Robin Hood by guile, he called his constables
together. "Now take ye each four men, all armed in
proof," said he, "and get ye gone to the forest, at
different points, and lay in wait for this same Robin
Hood. But if any constable finds too many men against
him, let him sound a horn, and then let each band
within hearing come with all speed and join the party
that calls them. Thus, I think, shall we take this green-
clad knave. Furthermore, to him that first meeteth
with Robin Hood shall one hundred pounds of silver
money be given if he be brought to me, dead or alive;
and to him that meeteth with any of his band shall
twoscore pounds be given, if such be brought to me
dead or alive. So, be ye bold and be ye crafty."

So thus they went in threescore companies of five

to Sherwood Forest, to take Robin Hood, each constable wishing that he might be the one to find the bold outlaw, or at least one of his band. For seven days and nights they hunted through the forest glades, but never saw so much as a single man in Lincoln green.

But early in the morning of the eighth day Robin Hood called the band together and said, "Now who will go and find what the Sheriff's men are at by this time? For I know right well they will not bide forever within Sherwood shades."

At this a great shout arose, and each man waved his bow aloft and cried that he might be the one to go. Then Robin Hood's heart was proud when he looked around on his stout, brave fellows, and he said, "Brave and true are ye all, my merry men, and a right stout band of good fellows are ye; but ye cannot all go, so I will choose one from amongst you, and it shall be good Will Stutely, for he is as sly as e'er an old dog fox in Sherwood Forest."

Then Will Stutely leaped high aloft and laughed loudly, clapping his hands, for pure joy that he should

have been chosen from amongst them all. "Now
thanks, good master," quoth he, "and if I bring not
news of those knaves to thee, call me no more thy sly
Will Stutely."

Then he clad himself in a friar's gown, and underneath the robe he hung a good broadsword in such a
place that he could easily lay hands upon it. Thus clad,
he set forth upon his quest, until he came to the verge
of the forest, and so to the highway.

At the Blue Boar Inn he found a band of the Sheriff's
men drinking right lustily; so, without speaking to
anyone, he sat down upon a distant bench, his staff in
his hand, and his head bowed forward as though he
were meditating.

As he sat thus, there came a great house-cat and
rubbed against his knee, raising his robe a palm's
breadth high. Stutely pushed his robe quickly down
again, but the constable who commanded the Sheriff's
men saw what had passed, and saw also fair Lincoln
green beneath the friar's robe. So, presently, he said
aloud:—

"Whither goest thou, holy friar, upon this hot summer's day?"

"I go a pilgrim to Canterbury Town," answered Will Stutely, speaking gruffly, so that none might know his voice.

Then the constable said, "Now tell me, holy father, do pilgrims to Canterbury wear good Lincoln green beneath their robes? Ha! by my faith, I take thee to be some lusty thief, and perhaps one of Robin Hood's own band! Now, by Our Lady's grace, if thou movest hand or foot, I will run thee through the body with my sword!"

Then he flashed forth his bright sword and leaped upon Will Stutely, thinking he would take him unaware; but Stutely had his own sword tightly held in his hand, beneath his robe, so he drew it forth before the constable came upon him. Then the stout constable struck a mighty blow; but he struck no more in all that fight, for Stutely, parrying the blow right deftly, smote the constable back again with all his might. Then he would have escaped, but could not, for the other, all dizzy with the wound and with the flowing blood, seized him by the knees with his arms even as he reeled and fell. Then the others rushed upon him, and Stutely struck again at another of the Sheriff's men, but the steel cap glanced the blow, and though the blade bit deep, it did not kill. Meanwhile, the constable, fainting as he was, drew Stutely downward, and the others, seeing the yeoman hampered so, rushed upon him again, and one smote him a blow upon the crown so that the blood ran down his face and blinded him. Then, staggering, he fell, and all sprang upon him, though he struggled so manfully that they could hardly hold him fast. Then they bound him with stout hempen cords so that he could not move either hand or foot, and thus they overcame him. But it was a doleful day's doings for two of that band; for the constable was sorely wounded, and the other, that Stutely smote upon the crown, lay sick for many a day ere he was the stout man that he had been before this famous fight.

Robin Hood stood under the greenwood-tree thinking of Will Stutely and how he might be faring, when suddenly he saw two of his stout yeomen come running down the forest path, and betwixt them ran buxom Maken of the Blue Boar. Then Robin's heart fell, for he knew they were the bearers of ill tidings.

"Will Stutely hath been taken," cried they, when they had come to where he stood.

"And is it thou that hast brought such doleful news?" said Robin to the lass.

"Ay, marry, for I saw it all," cried she, panting as the hare pants when it has escaped the hounds; "and I fear he is wounded sore, for one smote him main shrewdly i' the crown. They have bound him and taken him to Nottingham Town, and ere I left the Blue Boar I heard that he should be hanged to-morrow day."

"He shall not be hanged to-morrow day," cried Robin; "or, if he be, full many a one shall gnaw the sod, and many shall have cause to cry Alack-a-day!"

Then he clapped his horn to his lips and blew three blasts right loudly, and presently his good yeomen

came running through the greenwood until sevenscore
bold blades were gathered around him.

"Now hark you all!" cried Robin. "Our dear companion, Will Stutely, hath been taken by that vile
Sheriff's men, therefore doth it behoove us to take
bow and brand in hand to bring him off again; for I
wot that we ought to risk life and limb for him, as he
hath risked life and limb for us. Is it not so, my merry
men all?" Then all cried, "Ay!" with a great voice.

The sun was low in the western sky when a bugle-
note sounded from the castle wall. Then all was bustle
in Nottingham Town and crowds filled the streets, for
all knew that the famous Will Stutely was to be hanged
that day. Presently the castle gates opened wide and a
great array of men-at-arms came forth with noise and
clatter, the Sheriff, all clad in shining mail of linked
chain, riding at their head. In the midst of all the
guard, in a cart, with a halter about his neck, rode
Will Stutely. His face was pale with his wound and
with loss of blood, like the moon in broad daylight

and his fair hair was clotted in points upon his forehead, where the blood had hardened. When he came
forth from the castle he looked up and he looked down
but though he saw some faces that showed pity and
some that showed friendliness, he saw none that he
knew. So, at last, they came to the great town gate,
through which Stutely saw the fair country beyond,
with hills and dales all clothed in verdure, and far away
the dusky line of Sherwood's skirts. Then when he saw
the slanting sunlight lying on field and fallow, shining
redly here and there on cot and farm-house, and when
he heard the sweet birds singing their vespers, and the
sheep bleating upon the hill-side, and beheld the
swallows flying in the bright air, there came a great
fulness to his heart so that all things blurred to his
sight through salt tears, and he bowed his head lest the
folk should think him unmanly when they saw the
tears in his eyes. Thus he kept his head bowed till they
had passed through the gate and were outside the walls of
the town. But when he looked up again he felt his
heart leap within him and then stand still for pure joy,

for he saw the face of one of his own dear companions
of merry Sherwood; then glancing quickly around he
saw well-known faces upon all sides of him, crowding
closely upon the men-at-arms who were guarding him.
Then of a sudden the blood sprang to his cheeks, for he
saw for a moment his own good master in the press,
and, seeing him, knew that Robin Hood and all his
band were there. Yet betwixt him and them was a
line of men-at-arms.

"Now, stand back!" cried the Sheriff in a mighty
voice, for the crowd pressed around on all sides.
"What mean ye, varlets, that ye push upon us so?
Stand back, I say!"

Then came a bustle and a noise, and one strove to
push between the men-at-arms so as to reach the cart,
and Stutely saw that it was Little John that made all
that stir.

"Now stand thou back!" cried one of the men-at-
arms whom Little John pushed with his elbows.

"Now stand thou back thine own self," quoth Little
John, and straightway smote the man a buffet beside

his head that felled him as a butcher fells an ox, and then he leaped to the cart where Stutely sat.

"I pray thee take leave of thy friends ere thou diest, Will," quoth he, "or maybe I will die with thee if thou must die, for I could never have better company." Then with one stroke he cut the bonds that bound the other's arms and legs, and Stutely leaped straightway from the cart.

"Now as I live," cried the Sheriff, "yon varlet I know right well is a sturdy rebel! Take him, I bid you all, and let him not go!"

So saying he spurred his horse upon Little John, and rising in his stirrups smote with might and main, but Little John ducked quickly underneath the horse's belly and the blow whistled harmlessly over his head.

"Nay, good Sir Sheriff," cried he, leaping up again when the blow had passed, "I must e'en borrow thy most worshipful sword." Thereupon he twitched the weapon deftly from out the Sheriff's hand. "Here, Stutely," he cried, "the Sheriff hath lent thee his

sword! Back to back with me, man, and defend thyself, for help is nigh!''

''Down with them!'' bellowed the Sheriff in a voice
like an angry bull; and he spurred his horse upon the
two who now stood back to back, forgetting in his
rage that he had no weapon with which to defend
himself.

''Stand back, Sheriff!'' cried Little John; and even
as he spoke, a bugle-horn sounded shrilly, and a cloth-
yard shaft whistled within an inch of the Sheriff's head.
Then there came a swaying hither and thither and
oaths and cries and groans and clashing of steel, and
swords flashed in the setting sun, and a score of arrows
whistled through the air: and some cried ''Help,
help!'' and some, ''A rescue, a rescue!''

''Treason!'' cried the Sheriff in a loud voice. ''Bear
back! bear back! else we be all dead men!'' Thereupon he reined his horse backward through the thick-
est of the crowd.

Now Robin Hood and his band might have slain half
of the Sheriff's men had they desired to do so, but

they let them push out of the press and get them gone, only sending a bunch of arrows after them to hurry them in their flight.

"Oh, stay!" shouted Will Stutely after the Sheriff. "Thou wilt never catch bold Robin Hood if thou dost not stand to meet him face to face." But the Sheriff, bowing along his horse's back, made no answer but only spurred the faster.

Then Will Stutely turned to Little John and looked him in the face till the tears ran down from his eyes and he wept aloud, and kissing his friend's cheeks, "O Little John!" quoth he, "mine own true friend, that he that I love better than man or woman in all the world beside! Little did I reckon to see thy face this day, or to meet thee this side Paradise." And Little John could make no answer, but wept also.

Thus the Sheriff of Nottingham tried twice to take Robin Hood and failed each time; and the last time he was frightened, for he felt how near he had come to losing his life; so he said: "These men fear neither God nor man, nor King, nor king's officers. I would sooner lose mine office than my life, so I will trouble them no more.'' So he kept close within his castle for many a day and dared not show his face outside of his own household, and all the time he was gloomy and would speak to no one, for he was ashamed of what had happened that day.

CHAPTER IV

How Robin Hood
turned butcher

Now after all these things had happened, and it became
known to Robin Hood how the Sheriff had twice tried
to make him captive, he said to himself: "If I have the
chance, I will make our worshipful Sheriff pay right
well for that which he hath done to me. Maybe I may
bring him some time into Sherwood Forest, and have
him to a right merry feast with us." For when Robin
Hood caught a baron or a squire, or a fat abbot or
bishop, he brought them to the greenwood tree and
feasted them before he lightened their purses.

43

But in the meantime Robin Hood and his band
lived quietly in Sherwood Forest, without showing
their faces abroad, for Robin knew that it would not
be wise for him to be seen in the neighborhood of
Nottingham, those in authority being very wroth with
him. But though they did not go abroad, they lived a
merry life within the woodlands, spending the days in
shooting at garlands hung upon a willow wand at the
end of the glade, the leafy aisles ringing with merry
jests and laughter: for whoever missed the garland was
given a sound buffet, which, if delivered by Little
John, never failed to topple over the unfortunate yeoman. Then they had bouts of wrestling and of cudgel
play, so that every day they gained in skill and strength.

Thus they dwelt for nearly a year, and at last Robin
Hood began to fret at his confinement; so one day he
took up his stout cudgel and set forth to seek adventure, strolling blithely along until he came to the edge
of Sherwood. There, as he rambled along the sunlit
road, he met a lusty young butcher driving a fine mare,
and riding in a stout new cart, all hung about with
meat. Merrily whistled the butcher as he jogged along,

for he was going to the market, and the day was fresh
and sweet, making his heart blithe within him.

"Good-morrow to thee, jolly fellow," quoth
Robin; "now, where goest thou with thy meat, my
fair friend?"

"I go to the market at Nottingham Town to sell my
beef and my mutton," answered the butcher. "But
who art thou that comest from Locksley Town?"

"A yeoman am I, good friend, and men do call me
Robin Hood."

"Now, by Our Lady's grace," cried the butcher,
"well do I know thy name, and many a time have I
heard thy deeds both sung and spoken of. But heaven
forbid that thou shouldst take ought of me! An honest
man am I, and have wronged neither man nor maid;
so trouble me not, good master, as I have never
troubled thee."

"Nay, Heaven forbid, indeed," quoth Robin, "not
so much as one farthing would I take from thee, for I
love a fair Saxon face like thine."

Then he plucked the purse from his girdle, and
quoth he, "I would fain be a butcher for the day and

sell my meat in Nottingham Town, wilt thou close a
bargain with me and take six marks for thine outfit?"

"Now may the blessings of all the saints fall on thine
honest head!" cried the butcher right joyfully, as he
leaped down from his cart and took the purse that
Robin held out to him.

"Nay," quoth Robin, laughing loudly, "many do
like me and wish me well, but few call me honest."
So saying, he donned the butcher's apron, and, climb-
ing into the cart, he took the reins in his hand, and
drove off through the forest to Nottingham Town.

When he came to Nottingham, he entered that part
of the market where butchers stood, and took up his
inn in the best place he could find. Next, he opened
his stall and spread his meat upon the bench, then,
taking his cleaver and steel and clattering them together, he trolled aloud, in merry tones:—

> "Now come, ye lasses, and eke, ye dames,
>   And buy your meat from me;
> For three pennyworth of meat I sell
>   For the charge of one penny."

Thus he sang blithely, while all who stood near listened amazedly; then he clattered the steel and cleaver still more loudly, shouting lustily, "Now, who'll buy? who'll buy? Four fixed prices have I. Three pennyworths of meat I sell to the Lord Sheriff for sixpence, for I want not his custom; stout alderman I charge threepence, for it doth not matter to me whether they buy or not; to buxom dames I sell three pennyworths of meat for one penny, for I like their custom well; but to the bonny lass that hath a liking for a good tight butcher I charge naught but one fair kiss, for I like her custom best of all."

Then all began to stare and wonder, and crowd around, laughing, for he sold his meat so fast that no butcher that stood near him could sell anything.

Then they began to talk among themselves, and some said, "This must be some prodigal who hath sold his father's land, and would fain live merrily while the money lasts."

Then some of the butchers came to him to make his acquaintance. "Come, brother," quoth one who was the head of them all, "we be all of one trade, so

wilt thou go dine with us? For this day the Sheriff hath
asked all the Butcher Guild to feast with him at the
Guild Hall. There will be stout fare, and that thou
likest, or I much mistake thee."

"Now, beshrew his heart," quoth jolly Robin,
"that would deny a butcher. And, moreover, I will
go dine with you all, my sweet lads, and that as fast
as I can hie." Whereupon, having sold all his meat,
he closed his stall, and went with them to the great
Guild Hall.

There the Sheriff had already come in state, and
with him many butchers. When Robin and those that
were with him came in, all laughing at some merry
jest he had been telling them, those that were near
the Sheriff whispered to him, "Yon is a right mad
blade, for he hath sold more meat for one penny this
day than we could sell for three, and to whatsoever
merry lass gave him a kiss he gave meat for naught."
And others said, "He is some prodigal that hath sold
his land for silver and gold, and meaneth to spend all
right merrily."

Robin·turns·butcher·and·
sells·his·meat·in·Nottingham:

Then the Sheriff called Robin to him, not knowing him in his butcher's dress, and made him sit close to him on his right hand; for he loved a rich young prodigal—especially when he thought that he might lighten that prodigal's pockets into his own most worshipful purse. So he made much of Robin, and laughed and talked with him more than with any of the others.

At last the dinner was ready to be served and then Robin stood up and said:

"How now, brothers, be merry! nay, never count over your farthings, for by this and by that I will pay this shot myself, e'en though it cost two hundred pounds. So let no man draw up his lip, nor thrust his forefinger into his purse, for I swear that neither butcher nor Sheriff shall pay one penny for this feast."

"Now thou art a right merry soul," quoth the Sheriff, "and I wot thou must have many a head of horned beasts and many an acre of land, that thou dost spend thy money so freely."

"Ay, that have I," quoth Robin, laughing loudly

again, "five hundred and more horned beasts have I
and my brothers, and none of them have we been able
to sell, else I might not have turned butcher. As for
my land, I have never asked my steward how many
acres I have."

At this the Sheriff's eyes twinkled, and he chuckled
to himself. "Nay, good youth," quoth he, "if thou
canst not sell thy cattle it may be I will find a man
that will lift them from thy hands; perhaps that man
may be myself, for I love a merry youth and would
help such a one along the path of life. Now how much
dost thou want for thy horned cattle?"

"Well," quoth Robin, "they are worth at least
five hundred pounds."

"Nay," answered the Sheriff, slowly, and as if he
were thinking within himself, "well do I love thee,
and fain would I help thee along, but five hundred
pounds in money is a good round sum; beside I have
it not by me. Yet I will give thee three hundred pounds
for them all, and that in good hard silver and gold."

"Now thou old rogue!" quoth Robin; "well thou

knowest that so many horned cattle are worth seven
hundred pounds and more, and even that is but small
for them, and yet thou, with thy gray hairs and one
foot in the grave, wouldst trade upon the folly of a
wild youth.''

At this the Sheriff looked grimly at Robin. ''Nay,''
quoth Robin, ''look not on me as though thou hadst
sour beer in thy mouth, man. I will take thine offer,
for I and my brothers do need the money. We lead a
merry life, and no one leads a merry life for a farthing,
so I will close the bargain with thee. But mind that
thou bringest a good three hundred pounds with thee,
for I trust not one that driveth so shrewd a bargain.''

The afternoon had come when the Sheriff mounted
his horse and joined Robin Hood, who stood outside
the gateway of the paved court waiting for him, for
he had sold his horse and cart to a trader for two
marks. Then they set forth upon their way, the Sheriff
riding upon his horse and Robin running beside him.
Thus they left Nottingham Town and journeyed onward till they came within the forest shades, and the

deeper they went the more quiet grew the Sheriff.
For he began to bethink him that this was, maybe, a
neighborhood where the outlaw, Robin Hood, fre-
quented and well he knew what might happen to him
if he fell into the hands of that bold yeoman. So he
grew more and more quiet and peered this way and
that into the thickets as they rode deeper and deeper
into the shadows of the forest. At last they came to
where the road took a sudden bend, and before them
a herd of dun deer went tripping across the path.
Then Robin Hood came close to the Sheriff, and
pointing his finger he said: "These are my horned
beasts, good Master Sheriff. How dost thou like them?
Are they not fat and fair to see?"

At this the Sheriff drew rein quickly. "Now fellow," quoth he, "I would I were well out of this
forest, for I like not thy company. Go thou thine own
path, good friend, and let me but go mine."

But Robin only laughed and caught the Sheriff's
bridle rein. "Nay," cried he, "stay a while, for I
would thou shouldst see my brothers who own these

fair horned beasts with me." So saying he clapped his
bugle to his mouth and winded three merry notes,
and presently up the path came leaping fivescore good
stout yeoman with Little John at their head.

"What wouldst thou have, good master?" quoth
Little John.

"Why," answered Robin, "dost thou not see that
I have brought goodly company to feast with us to-day?
Fye, for shame! do you not see our good and worshipful master, the Sheriff of Nottingham? Take thou his
bridle, Little John, for he has honored us to-day by
coming to feast with us."

Then all doffed their hats humbly, without smiling,
or seeming to be in jest, whilst Little John took the
bridle rein and led the palfrey into the heart of the
forest, all marching in order, with Robin Hood walking beside the Sheriff, hat in hand.

All this time the Sheriff said never a word, but only
looked about him like one suddenly awakened from
sleep; but when he found himself going within the
very depth of Sherwood his heart sank within him,
for he thought, "Surely my three hundred pounds will

be taken from me, even if they take not my life itself, for I have plotted against their lives more than once." But all seemed humble and meek and not a word was said of danger, either to life or money.

So at last they came to that part of Sherwood Forest where a noble oak spread its branches wide, and beneath it was a seat all made of moss, on which Robin sat down, placing the Sheriff at his right hand. "Now busk ye, my merry men all," quoth he, "and bring forth the best we have, for his worship, the Sheriff, hath feasted me in Nottingham Guild-Hall to-day, and I would not have him go back empty."

All this time nothing had been said of the Sheriff's money, so presently he began to pluck up heart; "For," said he to himself, "maybe Robin Hood hath forgotten all about it."

Then, whilst beyond in the forest bright fires crackled and savory smells of sweetly roasting venison and fat capons filled the glade, and brown pasties warmed beside the blaze, did Robin Hood entertain the Sheriff right royally. First, several couples stood forth at quarterstaff, and so shrewd were they at the

game, and so quickly did they give stroke and parry,
that the Sheriff, who loved to watch all lusty sports of
the kind, clapped his hands, forgetting where he was,
and crying aloud, "Well struck! Well struck!"

Then the best archers of the band set up a fair
garland of flowers at eightscore paces distance, and
shot at it with the cunningest archery practice. But
the Sheriff grew grave, for he did not like this so well,
the famous meeting at the butts in Nottingham Town
being still green in his memory, and the golden arrow
that had been won there hanging close behind him.
Then, when Robin saw what was in the Sheriff's mind,
he stopped the sport, and called forth some of his
band, who sang merry ballads, while others made
music upon the harp.

When this was done, several yeomen came forward
and spread cloths upon the green grass, and placed a
royal feast. Then all sat down and feasted and drank
merrily together until the sun was low and the half-
moon glimmered with a pale light betwixt the leaves
of the trees overhead.

Then the Sheriff arose and said, "I thank you all, good yeomen, for the merry entertainment ye have given me this day. Right courteously have ye used me, showing therein that ye have much respect for our glorious King and his deputy in brave Nottingham-shire. But the shadows grow long, and I must away before darkness comes, lest I lose myself within the forest."

Then Robin Hood and all his merry men arose also, and Robin said to the Sheriff, "If thou must go, worshipful sir, go thou must; but thou hast forgotten one thing."

"Nay, I forgot naught," said the Sheriff; yet all the same his heart sank within him.

"But I say thou hast forgot something," quoth Robin. "We keep a merry inn here in the greenwood, but whoever becometh our guest must pay his reckon-ing."

Then the Sheriff laughed, but the laugh was hollow. "Well, jolly boys," quoth he, "we have had a merry time together to-day, and even if ye had not asked me,

I would have given you a score of pounds for the sweet entertainment I have had.''

"Nay,'' quoth Robin seriously, "it would ill beseem us to treat your worship so meanly. By my faith, Sir Sheriff, I would be ashamed to show my face if I did not reckon the King's deputy at three hundred pounds. Is it not so, my merry men all?''

Then "Ay!'' cried all, in a loud voice.

"Three hundred pounds!'' roared the Sheriff. "Think ye that your beggarly feast was worth three pounds, let alone three hundred?''

"Nay,'' quoth Robin, gravely. "Speak not so roundly, your worship. I do love thee for the sweet feast thou has given me this day in merry Nottingham Town; but there be those here who love thee not so much. If thou wilt look down the cloth thou wilt see Will Stutely, in whose eyes thou hast no great favor; then two other stout fellows are there here that thou knowest not, that were wounded in a brawl nigh Nottingham Town, some time ago—thou wottest when; one of them was sore hurt in one arm, yet he hath got the use of it again. Good Sheriff, be advised

by me; pay thy score without more ado, or maybe it
may fare ill with thee."

As he spoke the Sheriff's ruddy cheeks grew pale,
and he said nothing more but looked upon the ground
and gnawed his nether lip. Then slowly he drew forth
his fat purse and threw it upon the cloth in front of
him.

"Now take the purse, Little John," quoth Robin
Hood, "and see that the reckoning be right. We
would not doubt our Sheriff, but he might not like it
if he should find he had not paid his full score."

Then Little John counted the money, and found
that the bag held three hundred pounds in silver and
gold. But to the Sheriff it seemed as if every clink of
the bright money was a drop of blood from his veins;
and when he saw it all counted out in a heap of silver
and gold, filling a wooden platter, he turned away and
silently mounted his horse.

"Never have we had so worshipful a guest before!"
quoth Robin; "and, as the day waxeth late, I will
send one of my young men to guide thee out of the
forest depths."

"Nay, Heaven forbid!" cried the Sheriff, hastily. "I can find mine own way, good fellow, without aid."

"Then I will put thee on the right track mine own self," quoth Robin; and, taking the Sheriff's horse by the bridle rein, he led him into the main forest path; then, before he let him go he said, "Now, fare thee well, good Sheriff, and when next thou thinkest to despoil some poor prodigal, remember thy feast in Sherwood Forest. 'Ne'er buy a horse, good friend, without first looking into its mouth,' as our good Gaffer Swanthold says. And so, once more, fare thee well." Then he clapped his hand to the horse's back and off went nag and Sheriff through the forest glades.

Then bitterly the Sheriff rued the day that first he meddled with Robin Hood, for all men laughed at him and many ballads were sung by folk throughout the country, of how the Sheriff went to shear and came home shorn to the very quick. For thus men sometimes overreach themselves through greed and guile.

CHAPTER V

How Little John went
to the Fair at Nottingham Town

Now we will tell the merry adventures that befell Little John at the shooting-match at Nottingham, and how he overcame Eric o' Lincoln in the famous bout at quarterstaff in that town; also how he entered the Sheriff's service, and of his merry encounter with the Sheriff's cook. So listen to what follows.

Spring had gone since the Sheriff's feast in Sherwood, and summer also, and the mellow month of October had come. All the air was cool and fresh; the harvests were gathered home, the young birds were full fledged, the hops were plucked, and apples were ripe.

With October had come the time for holding the great Fair which was celebrated every five years at Nottingham Town, to which folk came from far and

near throughout the country. At such times archery
was always the main sport of the day, for the Nottinghamshire yeomen were the best hand at the longbow
in all Merry England; but this year the Sheriff proclaimed that a prize of two fat steers should be given
to the best bowman.

When Robin Hood heard what had been proclaimed
he was vexed, and said, "Now beshrew this Sheriff
that he should offer such a prize that none but shep-
herd hinds will care to shoot for it!"

Then up spoke Little John: "Nay, but hearken,
good master," said he, "I would fain go and strive to
win even this poor thing among the stout yeomen who
will shoot at Nottingham Town. All the disguise that
I wish is a good suit of scarlet instead of this of Lincoln
green. I will draw the cowl of my jacket about my
head so that it will hide my brown hair and beard, and
then, I trust, no one will know me."

So Little John clad himself all in scarlet, and started
off to the Fair at Nottingham Town.

Right merry were these Fair days at Nottingham,

when the green before the great town gate was dotted
with booths standing in rows, with tents of many-
colored canvas, hung about with streamers and garlands of flowers, and the folk came from all the
countryside, both gentle and common. In some booths
there was dancing to merry music, in others flowed
ale and beer, and in others yet again sweet cakes and
barley sugar were sold; and sport was going outside
the booths also, where some minstrel sang ballads of
the olden time, playing a second upon the harp, or
where the wrestlers struggled with one another within
the sawdust ring; but the people gathered most of all
around a raised platform where stout fellows played
at quarterstaff.

So Little John came to the Fair. All scarlet were his
hose and jerkin, and scarlet was his cowled cap, with
a scarlet feather stuck in the side of it. Over his
shoulders was slung a stout bow of yew, and across his
back hung a quiver of good round arrows. Many turned
to look after such a stout, tall fellow, for his shoulders
were broader by a palm's breadth than any that were

there, and he stood a head taller than all the other
men. The lasses, also, looked at him askance, thinking
they had never seen a lustier youth.

First of all Little John went to the dancing booth,
where three men made sweet music with bagpipes.
Here he laid aside his bow and his quiver, and joined
in the sport, dancing so long that none could stand
against him. A score of lasses came, one after another,
and strove to dance him down, but could not do so;
For Little John leaped so high, snapping his fingers the
while and shouted so loud, that every lass vowed, that
she had never seen so sweet a lad in all her life before.

Then, after he had danced a long time, he strolled
to the platform where they were at cudgel-play, for he
loved a bout at quarterstaff as he loved meat and drink;
and here befell an adventure that was sung in ballads
throughout the mid-country for many a day.

One fellow there was that cracked crowns of every
one who threw cap into the ring. This was Eric o'
Lincoln, of great renown, whose name had been sung
in ballads throughout the countryside. When Little

John reached the stand he found none fighting, but only bold Eric walking up and down the platform, swinging his staff and shouting lustily: "Now, who will come and stroke for the lass he loves the best, with a good Lincolnshire yeoman? How now, lads? step up! step up! or else the lasses' eyes are not bright hereabouts, or the blood of Nottingham youth is sluggish and cold. Lincoln against Nottingham, say I! for no one hath put foot upon the boards this day such as we of Lincoln call a cudgel-player."

At this, one would nudge another with his elbow, saying, "Go thou, Ned!" or "Go thou, Thomas!" but no lad cared to gain a cracked crown for nothing.

Presently Eric saw where Little John stood among the others, a head and shoulders above them all, and he called to him loudly, "Halloa, thou long-legged fellow in scarlet! Broad are thy shoulders and thick thy head; now, thou great lout, wilt thou not twirl staff for Nottingham?"

"Ay," quoth Little John, "it would pleasure me hugely to crack thy knave's pate, thou saucy braggart!

Now, is there never a man here that will lend me a
good stout staff till I try the mettle of yon fellow?''
At this, half a score reached him their staves, and he
took the stoutest and heaviest of them all. Thereupon
he cast the cudgel upon the stand, and, leaping lightly
after it, snatched it up in his hand again.

Then each man stood in his place and measured the
other with fell looks until he that directed the sport
cried, ''Play!'' At this they stepped forth, each grasp-
ing his staff tightly in the middle. Then those that
stood around saw the stoutest game of quarterstaff that
e'er Nottingham Town beheld. At first Eric o' Lincoln
thought that he would gain an easy advantage, so he
came forth as if he would say, ''Watch, good people,
how that I carve you this cockerel right speedily;''
but he presently found it to be no such speedy matter.
Right deftly he struck, and with great skill of fence,
but he had found his match in Little John. Once,
twice, thrice he struck, and three times Little John
turned the blows to the left hand and to the right.
Then quickly and with a dainty backhanded blow he

rapped Eric beneath his guard so shrewdly that it made his head ring again. Then Eric stepped back to gather his wits, while a great shout went up and all were glad that Nottingham had cracked Lincoln's crown; and thus ended the first bout of the game.

Then presently the director of the sport cried, "Play!" and they came together again; but now Eric played warily, for he found his man was of right good mettle, and also he had no sweet memory of the blow that he had got; so this bout neither Little John nor the Lincoln man caught a stroke within his guard; then, after a while, they parted again, and this made the second bout.

Then for the third time they came together, and at first Eric strove to be wary, as he had been before; but, growing mad at finding himself so foiled, he lost his wits, and began to rain blows so fiercely and so fast that they rattled like hail on penthouse roof; but, in spite of all, he did not reach within Little John's guard. Then at last Little John saw his chance and seized it right cleverly. Once more, with a quick blow,

he rapped Eric beside the head, and ere he could re-
gain himself, Little John slipped his right hand down
to his left, and, with a swinging blow, smote the other
so sorely upon the crown that down he fell as though
he would never move again.

Then the people shouted so loud that folk came
running from all about to see what was the ado; while
Little John leaped down from the stand and gave the
staff back to him that had lent it to him. And thus
ended the famous bout between Little John and Eric
o' Lincoln of great renown.

But now the time had come when those who were
to shoot with the longbow were to take their places,
so the people began flocking to the butts where the
shooting was to be. Near the target, in a good place,
sat the Sheriff, upon a raised dais, with many gentle-
folk around him. When the archers had taken their
places, the herald came forward and proclaimed the
rules of the game, and how each should shoot three
shots, and to him that should shoot the best the prize
of two fat steers was to belong. A score of brave shots
were gathered there, and among them some of the

Little·John·overcomes·Eric·o'·Lincoln

keenest hands at the longbow in Lincoln and Nottinghamshire; and among them Little John stood taller
than all the rest. "Who is yon stranger clad all in
scarlet?" said some; and others answered, "It is he
that hath but now so soundly cracked the crown of
Eric o' Lincoln." Thus the people talked among
themselves, until at last it reached even the Sheriff's
ears.

And now each man stepped forward and shot in
turn; but though each shot well, Little John was the
best of all, for three times he struck the clout, and
once only the length of a barleycorn from the centre.
"Hey for the tall archer!" shouted the crowd; and
some among them shouted, "Hey for Reynold Greenleaf!" for this was the name that Little John had
called himself that day.

Then the Sheriff stepped down from the raised seat
and came to where the archers stood, while all doffed
their caps that saw him coming. He looked keenly at
Little John, but did not know him, though he said,
after a while, "How now, good fellow, methinks there
is that about thy face that I have seen erewhile."

"Mayhap it may be so," quoth Little John, "for
often have I seen your worship;" and, as he spoke, he
looked steadily into the Sheriff's eyes, so that the
latter did not suspect who he was.

"A brave blade art thou, good friend," said the
Sheriff, "and I hear that thou hast well upheld the skill
of Nottinghamshire against that of Lincoln this day.
What may be thy name good fellow?"

"Men do call me Reynold Greenleaf, your worship," said Little John; and the old ballad that tells
of this, adds, "So, in truth, was he a green leaf, but
of what manner of tree the Sheriff wotted not."

"Now, Reynold Greenleaf," quoth the Sheriff,
"thou art the fairest hand at the longbow that mine
eyes ever beheld, next to that false knave, Robin
Hood, from whose wiles Heaven forfend me! Wilt
thou join my service, good fellow? Thou shalt be paid
right well, for three suits of clothes shalt thou have a
year, with good food! and, beside this, I will pay thee
forty marks each Michaelmastide."

"Then here stand I a free man, and right gladly will
I enter thy household," said Little John; for he

thought he might find some merry jest, should he enter the Sheriff's service.

"Fairly hast thou won the fat steers," said the Sheriff, "for, I wot, thou shootest as fair a shaft as Robin Hood himself."

"Then," said Little John, "for joy of having gotten myself into thy service, I will give the fat steers to all these good folk, to feast withal." At this arose a great shout, many casting their caps aloft, for joy of the gift.

Then some built great fires and roasted the steers, and all made themselves merry; and, when they had eaten and drunk as much as they could, and when the day faded and the great moon arose, all red and round, over the spires and towers of Nottingham Town, they joined hands and danced around the fires, to the music of bagpipes and harps. But long before this merry-making had begun, the Sheriff and his new servant, Reynold Greenleaf, were in the Castle of Nottingham.

CHAPTER VI

How Little John
left the Sheriff's service

Thus Little John entered into the Sheriff's service, and found the life he led there easy enough, for the Sheriff made him his right-hand man, and held him in great favor. He sat nigh the Sheriff at meat, and he ran beside his horse when he went a-hunting; so that, what with hunting and hawking a little, and eating rich dishes and sleeping until late hours in the morning, he grew as fat as a stall-fed ox.

One morning the Sheriff and many of his men set forth to meet certain lords, to go a-hunting. As for Little John, he lay abed, snoring lustily, till the sun was high in the heavens.

When he came down-stairs he saw the Steward standing near the pantry door,—a great, fat man, with a huge bundle of keys hanging to his girdle. Then Little John said, "Ho, Master Steward, a hungry man

am I, for naught have I had for all this blessed morn.
Therefore, give me to eat.''

Then the Steward looked grimly at him and rattled
the keys in his girdle. "So, Master Reynold Greenleaf, thou art an hungered, art thou?" quoth he. "But,
fair youth, if thou livest long enough, thou wilt find
that he who getteth overmuch sleep for an idle head
goeth with an empty stomach. For what sayeth the
old saw, Master Greenleaf? Is it not 'The late fowl
findeth but ill faring?' "

"Now, thou great purse of fat!" cried Little John,
"I ask thee not for fool's wisdom, but for bread and
meat. Who art thou, that thou shouldst deny me to
eat?" So saying, he strode to the pantry and tried to
open the door; but found it locked, whereat the
Steward laughed and rattled his keys again. Then the
wrath of Little John boiled over, and, lifting his
clenched fist, he smote the pantry door, bursting out
three panels, and making so large an opening that he
could easily stoop and walk through it.

When the Steward saw what was done, he waxed

mad with rage; and, as Little John stooped to look within the pantry, he seized him from behind by the nape of the neck, pinching him sorely and smiting him over the head with his keys till the yeoman's ears rang again. At this Little John turned upon the Steward and smote him such a buffet that the fat man fell to the floor and lay there as though he would never move again. "There," quoth Little John, "think well of that stroke and never keep a good breakfast from a hungry man again."

So saying, he crept into the pantry and looked about him to see if he could find something to appease his hunger. He saw a great venison pasty and two roasted capons, beside which was a platter of plover's eggs— a sweet sight to a hungry man. These he took down from the shelves and placed upon a sideboard, and prepared to make himself merry.

Now the Cook, in the kitchen across the courtyard, heard the loud talking between Little John and the Steward, and also the blow that Little John struck the other, so he came running across the court and up the

stairway to where the Steward's pantry was, bearing
in his hands the spit with the roast still upon it.
Meanwhile the Steward had gathered his wits about
him and risen to his feet, so that when the Cook came
to the Steward's pantry he saw him glowering through
the broken door at Little John, who was making ready
for a good repast. When the Steward saw the Cook, he
came to him, and putting one arm over his shoulder,
"Alas, sweet friend!" quoth he,—for the Cook was a
tall, stout man,—"seest thou what that vile knave,
Reynold Greenleaf, hath done? He hath broken in
upon our master's goods, and hath smitten me a
buffet upon the ear, so that I thought I was dead.
Good Cook, I love thee well; also I have ten shillings
that I mean to give as a gift to thee. But hatest thou not
to see a vile upstart like this Reynold Greenleaf taking
it upon him so bravely?"

"Ay, marry, that do I," quoth the Cook boldly,
for he liked the Steward because of his talk of the ten
shillings. "Get thee gone straightway to thy room,
and I will bring out this knave by his ears." So saying,

he laid aside his spit and drew the sword that hung by
his side; whereupon the Steward left as quickly as he
could, for he hated the sight of naked steel.

Then the Cook walked straightway to the broken
pantry door, through which he saw Little John tucking a napkin beneath his chin, and preparing to make
himself merry.

"Why, how now, Reynold Greenleaf?" said the
Cook; "thou art no better than a thief, I wot. Come
thou straight forth, man, or I will carve thee as I would
carve a sucking pig."

"Nay, good Cook, bear thou thyself more seem-
ingly, or else I will come forth to thy dole. At most
times I am as a yearly lamb, but when one cometh
between me and my meat, I am a raging lion, as it
were."

"Lion or no lion," quoth the valorous Cook,
"come thou straight forth, else thou art a coward
heart as well as a knavish thief."

"Ha!" cried Little John, "coward's name have I
never had; so, look to thyself, good Cook, for I come

forth straight, the roaring lion I did speak of but now."

Then he, too, drew his sword and came out of the pantry; then, putting themselves into position, they came slowly together, with grim and angry looks; but suddenly Little John lowered his point. "Hold, good Cook!" said he. "Now, I bethink me it were ill of us to fight with good victuals standing so nigh, and such a feast as would befit two stout fellows such as we are. Marry, good friend, I think we should enjoy this fair feast ere we fight. What sayest thou, jolly Cook?"

At this speech the Cook looked up and down, scratching his head in doubt, for he loved good feasting. At last he drew a long breath, and said to Little John, "Well, good friend, I like thy plan right well; so, pretty boy, say I, let us feast, with all my heart, for one of us may sup in Paradise before nightfall."

So each thrust his sword back into the scabbard, and entered the pantry; then, after they had seated themselves, Little John drew his dagger and thrust it into the pie. "A hungry man must be fed," quoth he, "so, sweet chuck, I help myself without leave." But

The·Mighty·Fight·betwixt:
Little·John·and·the·Cook:

the Cook did not lag far behind, for straightway his
hands also were deeply thrust within the goodly pasty.
After this, neither of them spoke further, but used
their teeth to better purpose. But though neither
spoke, they looked at one another, each thinking
within himself that he had never seen a more lusty
fellow than the one across the board.

At last, after a long time had passed, the Cook drew
a full, deep breath, as though of much regret, and
wiped his hands upon the napkin, for he could eat no
more. Little John, also, had enough, for he pushed
the pasty aside, as though he would say, "I want thee
by me no more, good friend."

"And now, Master Reynold Greenleaf," said the
Cook, "the day draweth on, and I have my cooking
to do ere our master cometh home; so let us e'en go
and settle this brave fight we have in hand."

"Ay, marry," quoth Little John, "and that right
speedily. Never have I been more laggard in fighting
than in eating. So come thou straight forth into the
passage-way, where there is good room to swing a
sword, and I will try to serve thee."

Then they both stepped forth into the broad passage
that led to the Steward's pantry, where each man drew
his sword again, and without more ado fell upon the
other as though he would hew his fellow limb from
limb. Then their swords clashed upon one another
with great din, and sparks flew from each blow in
showers. So they fought up and down the hall for an
hour and more, neither striking the other a blow,
though they strove their best to do so; for both were
skilful at the fence; so nothing came of all their labor.
Ever and anon they rested, panting; then, after getting
their wind, at it they would go again more fiercely
than ever. At last Little John cried aloud, "Hold,
good Cook!" whereupon each rested upon his sword,
panting.

"Now will I make my vow," quoth Little John,
"thou art the very best swordsman that ever mine
eyes beheld. Truly, I had thought to carve thee ere
now."

"And I had thought to do the same by thee," quoth
the Cook; "but I have missed the mark somehow."

"Now I have been thinking within myself," quoth
Little John, "what we are fighting for; but albeit I
do not rightly know."

"Why, no more do I," said the Cook. "I bear no
love for that pursy Steward, but I thought that we had
engaged to fight with one another, and that it must be
done."

"Now," quoth Little John, "it doth seem to me
that instead of striving to cut one another's throats,
it were better for us to be boon companions. What
sayest thou, jolly Cook, wilt thou go with me to
Sherwood Forest and join with Robin Hood's band?
Thou shalt live a merry life within the woodlands, and
sevenscore good companions shalt thou have, one of
whom is mine own self. Thou shalt have two suits of
Lincoln green each year, and forty marks in pay."

"Now, thou art a man after mine own heart!"
cried the Cook right heartily; "and, as thou speakest
of it, that is the very service for me. I will go with
thee, and that right gladly. Give me thy palm, sweet
fellow, and I will be thine own companion from henceforth. What may be thy name, lad?"

"Men do call me Little John, good fellow."

"How? And art thou indeed Little John, and Robin Hood's own right-hand man? Many a time and oft have I heard of thee, but never did I hope to set eyes upon thee. And thou art indeed the famous Little John!" And the Cook seemed lost in amazement, and looked upon his companion with open eyes.

"I am Little John, indeed, and I will bring to Robin Hood this day a right stout fellow to join his merry band. But ere we go, good friend, it seemeth to me to be a vast pity that, as we have had so much of the good Sheriff's food, we should not also carry off some of his silver plate to Robin Hood, as a present from his worship."

"Ay, marry is it," said the Cook. And so they began hunting about, and took as much silver as they could lay hands upon, clapping it into a bag, and when they had filled the sack they set forth to Sherwood Forest.

The Sheriff of Nottingham and a gay company were hunting near the forest. Suddenly Little John appeared before them and doffed his cap and bent his knee.

"God save thee, good master," quoth he.

"Why, Reynold Greenleaf!" cried the Sheriff, "whence cometh thou and where hast thou been?"

"I have been in the forest," answered Little John, speaking amazedly, "and there I saw a sight such as ne'er before man's eyes beheld! Yonder I saw a young hart all of green from top to toe, and about him was a herd of threescore deer, and they, too, were all of green from head to foot. Yet I dared not shoot, good master, for fear lest they should slay me."

"Why, how now, Reynold Greenleaf," cried the Sheriff; "art thou dreaming, or art thou mad, that thou dost bring me such a tale?"

"Nay, I am not dreaming nor am I mad," said Little John; "and if thou wilt come with me, I will show thee this fair sight, for I have seen it with mine own eyes. But thou must come alone, good master, lest the others frighten them and they make away."

So the party all rode forward, and Little John led them downward into the forest.

"Now, good master," quoth he at last, "we are nigh where I saw this herd."

Then the Sheriff descended from his horse and bade
them wait for him until he should return; and Little
John led him forward through a close copse until
suddenly they came to a great open glade, at the end
of which Robin Hood sat beneath the shade of the
great oak tree, with his merry men all about him.
"See, good master Sheriff," quoth Little John, "yonder is the hart of which I spake to thee."

At this the Sheriff turned to Little John, and said
bitterly, "Long ago I thought I remembered thy face,
but now I know thee. Woe betide thee, Little John,
for thou hast betrayed me this day."

Then Little John laughed aloud. "Good Master
Sheriff," said he, "thou dost indeed know me, and I
am Little John."

In the meantime Robin Hood had come to them.
"Now, welcome, Master Sheriff," he said. "Hast
thou come to take another feast with me?"

"Nay, Heaven forbid!" said the Sheriff, in tones of
deep earnest. "I care for no feast and have no hunger
to-day."

"I am grieved that thou wilt not feast with me,

Master Sheriff," quoth Robin, "for thou couldst have victuals to thy liking, for there stands thy Cook."

Then he led the Sheriff, will-he-nill-he, to the seat he knew so well beneath the greenwood tree.

"Ho, lads!" cried Robin, "fill our good friend, the Sheriff, a drink of refreshment and fetch it hither, for he is faint and weary."

Then one of the band brought the Sheriff a cup, bowing low as he handed it to him; but the Sheriff could not touch it, for he saw that it was one of his own silver flagons, served on one of his own silver plates.

"How now," quoth Robin, "dost thou not like our new silver service? We have gotten a bag of it this day." So saying, he held up the sack of silver that Little John and the Cook had brought with them.

Then the Sheriff's heart was bitter within him; but, not daring to say anything, he only gazed upon the ground. Robin looked keenly at him for a time before he spoke again; then said he, "Now, Master Sheriff, the last time thou camest to Sherwood Forest thou didst come seeking to despoil a poor spendthrift, and thou wert despoiled thine own self; but now thou comest seeking to do no harm, nor do I know that thou hast despoiled any man. I take my tithes from lordly squires, to help those that they despoil and to raise up those that they bow down; but I know not that thou hast tenants of thine own whom thou hast wronged in any way. Therefore, take thou thine own again; nor will I dispossess thee to-day of so much as one farthing. Come with me, and I will lead thee from the forest back to thine own party again."

Then, slinging the bag upon his shoulder, he turned away, the Sheriff following him, all too perplexed in mind to speak. So they went forward until they came to within a furlong of the spot where the Sheriff's companions were waiting for him. Then Robin Hood gave the sack of silver to the Sheriff. ''Take thou thine own again,'' he said, ''and, hearken to me, good Sheriff, take thou a piece of advice with it. Try thy servants well ere thou dost engage them again so readily.'' Then, turning, he left the other standing bewildered, with the sack in his hands.

The company that waited for the Sheriff were all

amazed to see him come out of the forest bearing a
heavy sack upon his shoulders; but though they
questioned him, he answered never a word, acting
like one who walks in a dream. Without a word, he
placed the bag across his nag's back, and then, mount-
ing, rode away, all following him; but all the time
there was a great turmoil of thoughts within his head,
tumbling one over the other. And thus ends the merry
tale of Little John and how he entered the Sheriff's
service.

CHAPTER VII

How Little John fought the Tanner of Blyth

One fine day, not long after Little John had left abiding with the Sheriff and had come back to the merry greenwood, Robin Hood and a few chosen fellows of his band lay upon the soft sward beneath the greenwood tree where they dwelt. The day was warm and sultry, so that whilst most of the band were scattered through the forest upon this mission and upon that, these few stout fellows lay lazily beneath the shade of the tree, in the soft afternoon, passing jests among themselves and telling merry stories, with laughter and mirth.

All the air was laden with the bitter fragrance of the
May, and all the bosky shades of the woodlands beyond
rang with the sweet song of birds,—the throstle-cock,
the cuckoo, and the wood-pigeon,—and with the song
of birds mingled the cool sound of the gurgling brook
that leaped out of the forest shades, and ran fretting
amid its rough, gray stones across the sunlit open
glade before the trysting-tree. And a fair sight was that
half-score of tall, stout yeomen, all clad in Lincoln
green, lying beneath the broad-spreading branches of
the great oak tree, amid the quivering leaves of which
the sunlight shivered and fell in dancing patches upon
the grass.

Suddenly Robin Hood smote his knee.

"By Saint Dunstan," quoth he, "I had nigh forgot
that quarter-day cometh on apace, and yet no cloth of
Lincoln green in all our store. It must be looked to,
and that in quick season. Come, busk thee, Little
John! stir those lazy bones of thine, for thou must get
thee straightway to our good gossip, the draper, Hugh
Longshanks of Ancaster. Bid him send us straightway

twentyscore yards of fair cloth of Lincoln green. Bide thou here till I bring thee money to pay our good Hugh. I warrant he hath no better customers in all Nottinghamshire than we." So saying, Robin left them and entered the forest.

Not far from the trysting-tree was a great rock in which a chamber had been hewn, the entrance being barred by a massive oaken door two palms' breadth in thickness, studded about with spikes, and fastened with a great padlock. This was the treasure-house of the band, and thither Robin Hood went, and, unlocking the door, entered the chamber, from which he brought forth a bag of gold, which he gave to Little John, to pay Hugh Longshanks withal, for the cloth of Lincoln green.

Then up got Little John, and, taking the bag of gold, which he thrust into his bosom, he strapped a girdle about his loins, took a stout pikestaff full seven feet long in his hand, and set forth upon his journey, Robin Hood going with him a part of the way for company's sake.

So they strode whistling along the leafy forest path
that led to Fosse Way, where, with a shake of the
hand, the two parted company, Little John jogging
upon his way and Robin Hood turning aside for a little
rest and a bit of gossip at the Blue Boar Inn.

Now, in the good town of Blyth there lived a stout
tanner, celebrated far and near for feats of strength
and many tough bouts at wrestling and the quarterstaff. For five years he had held the midcountry
champion belt for wrestling, till the great Adam o'
Lincoln cast him in the ring and broke one of his ribs;
but at quarterstaff he had never yet met his match in all
the country about. Beside all this, he dearly loved the
longbow, and a sly jaunt in the forest when the moon
was full and the dun deer in season; so that the King's
rangers kept a shrewd eye upon him and his doings,
for Arthur a Bland's house was apt to have a plenty of
meat in it that was more like venison than the law
allowed.

Now Arthur had been to Nottingham Town to sell
a halfscore of tanned cowhides. At the dawn of the day
he started homeward for Blyth. His way led, all in the

dewy morn, past the verge of Sherwood Forest, where the birds were welcoming the lovely day with a great and merry jubilee. Across the tanner's shoulders was slung his stout quarterstaff, ever near enough to him to be gripped quickly, and on his head was a cap of doubled cowhide, so tough that it could hardly be cloven even by a broadsword.

"Now," quoth Arthur a Bland to himself, when he had come to that part of the road that cut through a corner of the forest, "no doubt at this time of year the dun deer are coming from the forest depths nigher to the open meadow lands. Mayhap I may chance to catch a sight of the dainty brown darlings thus early in the morn." For there was nothing he loved better than to look upon a tripping herd of deer, even when he could not tickle their ribs with a clothyard shaft. Accordingly, quitting the path, he went peeping this way and that through the underbrush, spying now here and now there, with all the wiles of a master of wood-craft, and of one who had more than once donned a doublet of Lincoln green.

Now as Little John stepped blithely along, thinking

of nothing but of such things as the sweetness of the
hawthorn buds that bedecked the hedgerows, or the
crab-trees that stood here and there all covered with
fair pink blossoms, or gazing upward at the lark, that,
springing from the dewy grass, hung aloft on quivering
wings in the yellow sunlight, pouring forth its song
that fell like a falling star from the sky, his luck led
him away from the highway, not far from the spot
where Arthur a Bland was peeping this way and that
through the leaves of the thickets. Hearing a rustling
of the branches, Little John stopped, and presently
caught sight of the brown cowhide cap of the Tanner
moving amongst the bushes.

"I do much wonder," quoth Little John to himself, "what yon knave is after, that he should go thus
peeping and peering about. I verily believe that yon
scurvy varlet is no better than a thief, and cometh here
after our own and the good King's dun deer." For by
much roving in the forest, Little John had come to
look upon all the deer in Sherwood as belonging to
Robin Hood and his band as much as to good King

Harry. "Nay," quoth he again, after a time, "this matter must e'en be looked into." So, quitting the high-road, he also entered the thickets, and began spying around after stout Arthur a Bland.

So for a long time they both of them went hunting about, Little John after the Tanner, and the Tanner after the deer. At last Little John trod upon a stick, which snapped under his feet, whereupon, hearing the noise, the Tanner turned quickly and caught sight of the yeoman. Seeing that the Tanner had spied him out, Little John put a bold face upon the matter.

"Hilloa," quoth he, "what are thou doing here, thou naughty fellow? Who art thou that comest ranging Sherwood's paths? In very sooth thou hast an evil cast of countenance, and I do think, truly, that thou art no better than a thief, and comest after our good King's deer."

"Nay," quoth the Tanner boldly, for, though taken by surprise, he was not a man to be frightened by big words,—"thou liest in thy teeth. I am no thief, but an honest craftsman. As for my countenance, it is

what it is; and, for the matter of that, thine own is
none too pretty, thou saucy fellow."

"Ha!" quoth Little John, in a great loud voice,
"wouldst thou give me back-talk? Now I have a great
part of a mind to crack thy pate for thee. I would have
thee know, fellow, that I am, as it were, one of the
King's foresters. Leastwise," muttered he to himself,
"I and my friends do take good care of our good
sovereign's deer."

"I care not who thou art," answered the bold
Tanner, "and unless thou hast many more of thy kind
by thee, thou canst never make Arthur a Bland cry 'A
mercy.'"

"Is it so?" cried Little John, in a rage. "Now, by
my faith, thou saucy rogue, thy tongue hath led thee
into a pit thou wilt have a sorry time getting out of;
for I will give thee such a drubbing as ne'er hast thou
had in all thy life before. Take thy staff in thy hand,
fellow, for I will not smite an unarmed man."

"Marry come up with a murrain!" cried the Tanner, for he, too, had talked himself into a fume. "Big

words ne'er killed so much as a mouse. Who art thou
that talkest so freely of cracking the head of Arthur a
Bland? If I do not tan thy hide this day as ne'er I tanned
a calf's hide in all my life before, split my staff into
skewers for lamb's flesh and call me no more brave
man! Now look to thyself, fellow!"

"Stay!" said Little John; "let us first measure our
cudgels. I do reckon my staff longer than thine, and
I would not take vantage of thee by even so much as
an inch."

"Nay, I pass not for length," answered the Tanner.
"My staff is long enough to knock down a calf; so look
to thyself, fellow, I say again."

So, without more ado, each gripped his staff in the
middle, and, with fell and angry looks, they came
slowly together.

At about this time Robin Hood was returning homeward again from the Blue Boar. As he jogged along the
leafy road he heard, of a sudden, loud and angry voices,
as of men in a rage, passing fell words back and forth

from one to the other. At this, Robin Hood stopped
and listened. "Surely," quoth he to himself, "that is
Little John's voice, and he is talking in anger also.
Methinks the other is strange to my ears. Now Heaven
forfend that my good trusty Little John should have
fallen into the hands of the King's rangers. I must see
to this matter, and that quickly."

So, cautiously, he made his way through the thickets
whence the voices came, and, pushing aside the leaves,
peeped into the little open space where the two men,
staff in hand, were coming slowly together. "Ha!"
quoth Robin to himself, "here is merry sport afoot,
and no harm to anybody!" So saying, and being himself
yet unseen, he crept privily beneath a spreading bush
and stretched himself at length upon the ground, that
he might not only see the better, but that he might
enjoy the merry sight at his ease.

As you may have seen two dogs that think to fight,
walking slowly round and round each other, neither
cur wishing to begin the combat, so those two stout
yeomen moved slowly around, each watching for a
chance to take the other unaware, and so get in the

The·stout·bout·between·Little·Iohn·&·
Arthvr·a·Bland:·

first blow. At last Little John struck like a flash, and, "rap," the Tanner met the blow and turned it aside, and then smote back at Little John, who also turned the blow; and so this mighty battle began. Then up and down and back and forth they trod, the blows falling so thick and fast that, at a distance, one would have thought that half a score of men were fighting. Thus they fought for nigh half an hour, until the ground was all ploughed up with the digging of their heels, and their breathing grew labored like the ox in the furrow. But Little John suffered the most, for he had become unused to such stiff labor, and his joints were not as supple as they had been before he went to dwell with the Sheriff.

All this time Robin Hood lay beneath the bush, rejoicing at such a comely bout of quarterstaff. "By my faith!" quoth he to himself, "never had I thought to see Little John so evenly matched in all my life. Belike, though, he would have overcome yon stout fellow before this, had he been in his former trim."

At last Little John saw his chance, and, throwing

all the strength he felt going from him into one blow
that might have felled an ox, he struck at the Tanner
with might and main. And now did the Tanner's cowhide cap stand him in good stead, and but for it he
might never have held his staff in hand again. As it
was, the blow he caught beside the head was so
shrewd that it sent him staggering across the little
glade, so that, if Little John had had his old quickness
to follow up his vantage, it would have been ill for
stout Arthur. But he regained himself quickly, and, at
arm's length, struck back a blow at Little John, and
this time the stroke reached its mark, and down went
Little John at full length, his cudgel flying from his
hand as he fell. Then, raising his staff, stout Arthur
dealt him another blow upon the ribs.

"Hold!" roared Little John. "Wouldst thou strike
a man when he is down?"

"Ay, marry, would I," quoth the Tanner, giving
him another thwack with his staff.

"Stop!" roared Little John. "Help! hold, I say!
I yield me! I yield me, I say, good fellow!"

"Hast thou had enough?" asked the Tanner, grimly, holding his staff aloft.

"Ay, marry, and more than enough."

"And thou dost own that I am the better man of the two?"

"Yea, truly, and a murrain seize thee!" said Little John, the first aloud and the last to his beard.

"Then thou mayest go thy ways; and thank thy patron saint that I am a merciful man," said the Tanner.

"A plague o' such mercy as thine!" said Little John, sitting up and feeling his ribs where the Tanner had cudgelled him. "I make my vow, my ribs feel as though every one of them were broken in twain. I tell thee, good fellow, I did think there was never a man in all Nottinghamshire could do to me what thou hast done this day."

"And so thought I, also," cried Robin Hood, bursting out of the thicket and shouting with laughter till the tears ran down his cheeks. "O man, man!" said he, as well as he could for his mirth, " ' 'a did go

over like a little bottle knocked from a wall. I did see
the whole merry bout, and never did I think to see
thee yield thyself so, hand and foot, to any man in all
merry England. Marry, 'a did reach out his arm full
length whilst thou stood gaping at him, and, with a
pretty rap, tumbled thee over as never have I seen one
tumbled before." So spoke bold Robin, and all the
time Little John sat upon the ground, looking as
though he had sour curds in his mouth. "What may be
thy name, good fellow," said Robin, next, turning to
the Tanner.

"Men do call me Arthur a Bland," spoke up the
Tanner, boldly; "and now what may be thy name?"

"Ha, Arthur a Bland!" quoth Robin, "I have heard
thy name before, good fellow. Thou didst break the
crown of a friend of mine at the fair at Ely last October.
The folk there call him Jock o' Nottingham; we call
him Will Scathelock. This poor fellow whom thou
hast so belabored is counted the best hand at the
quarterstaff in all merry England. His name is Little
John, and mine Robin Hood."

"How!" cried the Tanner, "art thou indeed the
great Robin Hood, and is this the famous Little John?
Marry, had I known who thou art, I would never have
been so bold as to lift my hand against thee. Let me
help thee to thy feet, good Master Little John, and let
me brush the dust from off thy coat."

"Nay," quoth Little John, testily, at the same time
rising carefully, as though his bones had been made of
glass, "I can help myself, good fellow, without thy
aid; and, let me tell thee, had it not been for that vile
cowskin cap of thine, it would have been ill for thee
this day."

At this Robin laughed again, and, turning to the
Tanner, he said, "Wilt thou join my band, good
Arthur? for I make my vow thou art one of the stout-
est men that ever mine eyes beheld."

"Will I join thy band?" cried the Tanner, joyfully;
"ay, marry, will I! Hey for a merry life!" cried he,
leaping aloft and snapping his fingers, "and hey for the
life I love! Away with tanbark and filthy vats and foul
cowhides! I will follow thee to the ends of the earth,

good master, and not a herd of dun deer in all the forest but shall know the sound of the twang of my bowstring."

Thereupon, leaving the thickets, they took once more to the highway, and departed upon their business.

CHAPTER VIII

How Robin Hood fell in with Will Scarlet

After they had travelled some distance, the day being warm and the road dusty, Robin Hood waxed thirsty; so, there being a fountain of water as cold as ice, just behind the hedgerow, they crossed the stile and came to where the water bubbled up from beneath a mossy stone. Here, kneeling and making cups of the palms of their hands, they drank their fill, and then, the spot being cool and shady, they stretched their limbs and rested them for a space.

In front of them, over beyond the hedge, the dusty road stretched away across the plain; behind them the meadow lands and bright green fields of tender young corn lay broadly in the sun, and overhead spread the shade of the cool, rustling leaves of the beechen tree. Pleasantly to their nostrils came the tender fragrance of the purple violets and wild thyme that grew within

the dewy moisture of the edge of the little fountain,
and pleasantly came the soft gurgle of the water; all
else was sunny silence, broken only now and then by
the crow of a distant cock, borne up to them on the
wings of the soft and gentle breeze, or the drowsy
drone of the bumble-bee burrowing in the clover
blossoms that grew in the sun, or the voice of the busy
housewife in the nearest farmhouse. All was so pleas-
ant and so full of the gentle joy of the bright Maytime,
that for a long time neither of the three cared to speak,
but each lay on his back, gazing up through the trembling leaves of the trees to the bright sky overhead.
At last, Robin, whose thoughts were not quite so busy
woolgathering as those of the others, and who had
been gazing around him now and then, broke the
silence.

"Heyday!" quoth he, "yon is a gayly-feathered bird,
I take my vow."

The others looked and saw a young man walking
slowly down the highway. Gay was he, indeed, as
Robin had said, and a fine figure he cut, for his

doublet was of scarlet silk and his hosen also; a hand-
some sword hung by his side, the embossed leathern
scabbard being picked out with fine threads of gold;
his cap was of scarlet velvet, and a broad feather hung
down behind and back of one ear. His hair was long
and yellow and curled upon his shoulders, and in his
hand he bore an early rose, which he smelt at daintily
now and then.

"By my life!" quoth Robin Hood, laughing, "saw
ye e'er such a pretty, mincing fellow?"

"Truly, his clothes have overmuch prettiness for
my taste," quoth Arthur a Bland; "but, ne'ertheless,
his shoulders are broad and his loins are narrow and
seest thou, good master, how that his arms hang from
his body? They dangle not down like spindles, but
hang stiff and bend at the elbow. I take my vow, there
be no bread and milk limbs in those fine clothes, but
stiff joints and tough thews."

"Methinks thou art right, friend Arthur," said
Little John. "I do verily think that yon is no such
rose-leaf and whipped cream gallant as he would have

one take him to be. Besides, I wonder who he may be. Methinks yon fellow's hair is over light for Norman locks. He may be a good man and true for aught we know."

"Nay," said Robin, "my head against a leaden farthing, he is a Norman fop. Whenever saw ye Saxon mince along like that, as though he feared to muddy the toes of his shoes? At least, I will go forth and stop him, and see whether his purse be free of foul money. If I am wrong, then he may go forward upon his journey without the loss of much as a groat; but if I am right, I will pluck him as close as ever a goose was plucked for live feathers in midsummer. Thou sayst he is a sturdy fellow, Little John. Lie thou here and watch till I show thee how woodland life toughens a man, as easy living, such as thine of late with the Sheriff, drags him down. So, lie ye both here, I say, till I show you how I drub this fellow." So saying, Robin Hood stepped forth from the shade of the beech tree, crossed the stile, and stood in the middle of the road, in the stranger's path.

Meantime the stranger, who had been walking so slowly that all this talk was held before he came opposite the place where they were, neither quickened his pace nor seemed to see that such a man as Robin Hood was in the world. So Robin stood in the middle of the road, waiting while the other walked slowly forward, smelling his rose, and looking this way and that, and everywhere except at Robin.

"Hold!" cried Robin, when at last the other had come close to him. "Hold! stand where thou art!"

"Wherefore should I hold, good fellow?" said the stranger in soft and gentle voice; "and wherefore should I stand where I am? Ne'ertheless, as thou dost desire that I should stay, I will abide for a short time, that I may hear what thou mayst have to say to me."

"Then," quoth Robin, "as thou dost so fairly do as I tell thee, and dost give me such soft speech, I will also treat thee with all due courtesy. I would have thee know, fair friend, that I am, as it were, a sort of tax gatherer and levy a certain toll, which I use for purposes best known to myself. Therefore, sweet

Merry·Robin·stops·a·Stranger·in·Scarlet :·

chuck, I would have thee deliver to me thy purse, that I may look into it, and judge, to the best of my poor powers, whether thou hast more wealth about thee than our law allows."

All this time the youth had been sniffing at the rose that he held betwixt his thumb and finger. "Nay," said he with a gentle smile, when Robin Hood had done, "I do love to hear thee talk, thou pretty fellow, and if, haply, thou art not yet done, finish, I beseech thee. I have yet some little time to stay."

"I have said all," quoth Robin; "and now, if thou wilt give me thy purse, I will let thee go thy way without let or hindrance so soon as I shall see what it may hold. I will take none from thee if thou hast but little."

"Alas! it doth grieve me much," said the other, "that I cannot do as thou dost wish. I have nothing to give thee. Let me go my way, I prythee. I have done thee no harm."

"Nay, thou goest not," quoth Robin, "till thou hast shown me thy purse."

"Good friend," said the other, gently, "I have business elsewhere. I have given thee much time and have heard thee patiently. Prythee, let me now depart in peace."

"I have spoken to thee, friend," said Robin sternly, "and I now tell thee again, that thou goest not one step forward till thou hast done as I bid thee." So saying he raised his quarterstaff above his head in a threatening way.

"Alas!" said the stranger, sadly, "it doth grieve me that this thing must be. I fear much that I must slay thee, thou poor fellow!" So saying, he drew his sword.

"Put by thy weapon," quoth Robin; "I would take no vantage of thee. Thy sword cannot stand against an oaken staff such as mine. I could snap it like a barley straw. Yonder is a good oaken thicket by the roadside; take thee a cudgel thence and defend thyself fairly, if thou hast a taste for a sound drubbing."

First the stranger measured Robin with his eye, and then he measured the oaken staff. "Thou art right,

good fellow," said he, presently; "truly, my sword is
no match for that cudgel of thine. Bide thee a while
till I get me a staff." So saying, he threw aside the rose
that he had been holding all this time, thrust his sword
back into the scabbard, and, with a more hasty step
than he had yet used, stepped to the roadside where
grew the little clump of ground oaks Robin had spoken
of. Choosing among them, he presently found a sapling
to his liking. He did not cut it, but, rolling up his
sleeves a little way, he laid hold of it, placed his heel
against the ground, and, with one mighty pull, plucked
the young tree up by the roots from out the very
earth. Then he came back, trimming away the roots
and tender stems with his sword as quietly as if he had
done naught to speak of.

Little John and the Tanner had been watching all
that passed, but when they saw the stranger drag the
sapling up from the earth, and heard the rending and
snapping of its roots, the Tanner pursed his lips together, drawing his breath between them in a long
inward whistle.

"By the breath of my body!" said Little John, as
soon as he could gather his wits from their wonder,
"sawest thou that, Arthur? Marry, I think our poor
master will stand but an ill chance with yon fellow.
By Our Lady, he plucked up yon green tree as it were
a barley straw."

Whatever Robin Hood thought, he stood his ground,
and now he and the stranger in scarlet stood face to
face.

Well did Robin Hood hold his own that day as a
midcountry yeoman. This way and that they fought,
and back and forth, Robin's skill against the stranger's
strength. The dust of the highway rose up around
them like a cloud, so that at times Little John and the
Tanner could see nothing, but only hear the rattle of
the staves against one another. Thrice Robin Hood
struck the stranger; once upon the arm and twice
upon the ribs, and yet had he warded all the other's
blows, only one of which, had it met its mark, would
have laid stout Robin lower in the dust than he had
ever gone before. At last the stranger struck Robin's

cudgel so fairly in the middle that he could hardly hold his staff in his hand; again he struck, and Robin bent beneath the blow; a third time he struck, and now not only fairly beat down Robin's guard, but gave him such a rap, also, that down he tumbled into the dusty road.

"Hold!" cried Robin Hood, when he saw the stranger raising his staff once more. "I yield me!"

"Hold!" cried Little John, bursting from his cover, with the Tanner at his heels. "Hold! give over, I say!"

"Nay," answered the stranger, quietly, "if there be two more of you, and each as stout as this good fellow, I am like to have my hands full. Nevertheless, come on, and I will strive my best to serve you all."

"Stop!" cried Robin Hood, "we will fight no more. "Take my vow, this is an ill day for thee and me, Little John. I do verily believe that my wrist, and eke my arm, are palsied by the jar of the blow that this stranger struck me."

Then Little John turned to Robin Hood. "Why, how now, good master," said he; "alas! thou art in

an ill plight. Marry, thy jerkin is all befouled with the
dust of the road. Let me help thee to arise.''

"A plague on thy aid!" cried Robin, angrily. "I
can get to my feet without thy help, good fellow.''

"Nay, but let me at least dust thy coat for thee. I
fear thy poor bones are mightily sore," quoth Little
John, soberly, but with a sly twinkle in his eyes.

"Give over, I say!" quoth Robin in a fume.

"My coat hath been dusted enough already, without aid of thine." Then, turning to the stranger, he
said, "What may be thy name, good fellow?''

"My name is Gamwell," answered the other.

"Ha!" cried Robin, "is it even so? I have near kin
of that name. Whence camest thou, fair friend?''

"From Maxfield Town I come," answered the
stranger. "There was I born and bred, and thence I
come to seek my mother's young brother, whom men
call Robin Hood. So, if perchance thou mayst direct
me——''

"Ha! Will Gamwell!" cried Robin, placing both
hands upon the other's shoulders and holding him off

at arm's length. "Surely, it can be none other! I might have known thee by that pretty maiden air of thine,— that dainty, finicking manner of gait. Dost thou not know me, lad? Look upon me well."

"Now, by the breath of my body!" cried the other, "I do believe from my heart that thou art mine own Uncle Robin. Nay, certain it is so!" and each flung his arms around the other, kissing him upon the cheek.

"But tell me," said Robin Hood, "how camest thou to leave Sir Edward and thy mother?"

"Alas!" answered young Gamwell, "it is an ill story, uncle, that I have to tell thee. My father's steward, who came to us after old Giles Crookleg died, was ever a saucy varlet, and I know not why my father kept him, saving that he did oversee with great judgment. It used to gall me to hear him speak up so boldly to my father, who, thou knowest, was ever a patient man to those about him, and slow to anger and harsh words. Well, one day—and an ill day it was for that saucy fellow—he sought to berate my father, I standing by. I could stand it no longer, good uncle, so,

stepping forth, I gave him a box o' the ear, and—
wouldst thou believe it?—the fellow straightway died
o't. I think they said I broke his neck, or something
o' the like. So off they packed me to seek thee and
escape the law. I was on my way when thou sawest
me, and here I am.''

"Well, by the faith of my heart," quoth Robin
Hood, "for any one escaping the law thou wast taking
it the most easily that ever I beheld in all my life.
Whenever did any one in all the world see one who
had slain a man, and was escaping because of it, tripping along the highway like a dainty court damsel,
sniffing at a rose the while? But indeed I am right glad
to see thee, Will, and thou wilt add great honor and
credit to my band of merry fellows. But thou must
change thy name, for warrants will be out presently
against thee, so, because of thy gay clothes, thou shalt
henceforth and for aye be called Will Scarlet."

"Will Scarlet," quoth Little John, stepping forward and reaching out his great palm, which the other
took, "Will Scarlet, the name fitteth thee well. Right

glad am I to welcome thee amongst us. I am called Little John; and this is a new member who has just joined us, a stout tanner named Arthur a Bland. Thou art like to achieve fame, Will, let me tell thee, for there will be many a merry ballad sung about the country, and many a merry story told in Sherwood of how Robin Hood taught Little John and Arthur a Bland the proper way to use the quarterstaff; likewise, as it were, how our good master bit off so large a piece of cake that he choked on it."

"Come," cried Robin, biting his nether lip, while the others could not forbear laughing, "We will go no farther to-day, but will return to Sherwood, and thou shalt go to Ancaster another time, Little John."

So said Robin, for now that his own bones were sore, he felt as though a long journey would be an ill thing for them. So, turning their backs, they retraced their steps whence they came.

CHAPTER IX

The Merry Adventure
with Midge the Miller

When the four yeomen had travelled for a long time toward Sherwood again, high noontide being past, they began to wax hungry. Quoth Robin Hood, "I would that I had somewhat to eat. Methinks a good loaf of white bread, with a piece of snow-white cheese, were a feast for a king."

"Since thou speakest of it," said Will Scarlet, "methinks it would not be amiss myself. There is that within me crieth out, 'Victuals, good friend, victuals!' "

"I know a house near by," said Arthur a Bland, "and, had I but the money, I would bring ye that ye speak of; to wit, a sweet loaf of bread, and a fair cheese."

"For the matter of that, thou knowest I have money by me, good master," quoth Little John.

"Why, so thou hast, Little John," said Robin.

"How much money will it take, good Arthur, to buy us meat and drink?"

"I think that six broad pennies will buy food enow for a dozen men," said the Tanner.

"Then give him six pennies, Little John," quoth Robin, "for methinks food for three men will about fit my need. Now get thee gone, Arthur, with the money, and bring the food here, for there is a sweet shade in that thicket yonder, beside the road, and there will we eat our meal."

So Little John gave Arthur the money, and the others stepped to the thicket, there to await the return of the Tanner.

After a time he came back, bearing with him a great brown loaf of bread and a fair, round cheese. Then Will Scarlet took his sword and divided the loaf and the cheese into four fair portions, and each man helped himself.

After this no man spake more, but each munched away at his bread and cheese lustily.

At last Will Scarlet looked at a small piece of bread

he still held in his hand, and quoth he, "Methinks I
will give this to the sparrows." So, throwing it from
him, he brushed the crumbs from his jerkin.

"I, too," quoth Robin, "have had enough, I
think." As for Little John and the Tanner, they had
by this time eaten every crumb of their bread and
cheese.

"But, tell me," said Robin, "who may yon fellow
be coming along the road? Look, Little John, I pray,
and see if thou knowest him."

Little John looked whither Robin Hood pointed.
"Truly," quoth he, after a time, "I think yon fellow
is a certain young miller I have seen now and then
around the edge of Sherwood."

"Now thou speakest of him," quoth Robin Hood,
"methinks I myself have seen him now and then.
Hath he not a mill over beyond Nottingham Town,
nigh to the Salisbury road?"

"Thou art right; that is the man," said Little John.

"A good stout fellow," quoth Robin. "I saw him
crack Ned o' Bradford's crown about a fortnight

since, and never saw I hair lifted more neatly in all
my life before."

By this time the young miller had come so near that
they could see him clearly. His clothes were dusted
with flour, and over his back he carried a great sack of
meal, bending so as to bring the whole weight upon
his shoulders, and across the sack was a thick quarterstaff. His limbs were stout and strong, and he strode
along the dusty road right sturdily with the heavy sack
across his shoulders. His cheeks were ruddy as a winter hip, his hair was flaxen in color, and on his chin
was a downy growth of flaxen beard.

"A good honest fellow," quoth Robin Hood, "and
such an one as is a credit to English yeomanrie. Now
let us have a merry jest with him. We will forth as
though we were common thieves and pretend to rob
him of his honest gains. Then will we take him into
the forest and give him a feast such as he never had in
all his life before. Thereafter we will send him home
with crowns in his purse for every penny he hath.
What say ye, lads?"

"Truly, it is a merry thought," said Will Scarlet.

"It is well planned," quoth Little John, "but all the saints preserve us from any more drubbings this day! Marry, my poor bones ache so that I"—

"Prythee peace, Little John," quoth Robin. "Thy foolish tongue will get us both well laughed at yet should these adventures get talked abroad."

"My foolish tongue, forsooth," growled Little John to Arthur a Bland. "I would it could keep our master from getting us into another coil this day."

But now the Miller, plodding along the road, had come opposite to where the yeomen lay hidden, whereupon all four of them ran at him and surrounded him.

"Hold, friend!" cried Robin to the Miller, whereupon he turned slowly, with the weight of the bag upon his shoulder, and looked at each in turn all bewildered, for though a good stout man his wits did not skip like roasting chestnuts.

"Who bids me stay?" said the Miller in a voice deep and gruff, like the growl of a great dog.

"Marry that do I," quoth Robin; "and let me tell thee, friend, thou hadst best mind my bidding."

"And who art thou, good friend?" said the Miller, throwing the great sack of meal from his shoulder to the ground; "and who are those with thee?"

"We be four good Christian men," quoth Robin, "and would fain help thee by carrying part of thy heavy load for thee."

"I give you all thanks," said the Miller, "but my bag is none that heavy that I cannot carry it e'en by myself."

"Nay, thou dost mistake," quoth Robin, "I meant that thou mightest perhaps have some heavy farthings or pence about thee, not to speak of silver and gold. Our good Gaffer Swanthold sayeth that gold is an over heavy burden for a two-legged ass to carry; so we would e'en lift some of this load from thee."

"Alas!" cried the Miller; "what would ye do to me? I have not about me so much as a clipped groat. Do me no harm, I pray you, but let me depart in peace. Moreover, let me tell you that ye are upon Robin

Hood's ground, and should he find you seeking to rob
an honest craftsman, he will clip your ears to your
heads and scourge you even to the walls of Nottingham."

"In truth I fear Robin Hood no more than I do
myself," quoth jolly Robin. "Thou must this day give
up to me every penny thou hast about thee. Nay, if
thou dost budge an inch I will rattle this staff about
thine ears."

"Nay, smite me not!" cried the Miller, throwing
up his elbow as though he feared the blow. "Thou
mayst search me if thou wilt, but thou wilt find
nothing upon me, pouch, pocket, or skin."

"Is it so?" quoth Robin Hood, looking keenly
upon him. "Now I believe that what thou tellest is no
true tale. If I am not much mistook thou hast somewhat
in the bottom of that fat sack of meal. Good Arthur,
empty the bag upon the ground; I warrant thou wilt
find a shilling or two in the flour."

"Alas!" cried the Miller, falling upon his knees,
"spoil not all my good meal! It can better you not,

and will ruin me. Spare it, and I will give up the money in the bottom of the bag."

"Ha!" quoth Robin, nudging Will Scarlet, "Is it so? And have I found where thy money lies? Marry, I have a wondrous nose for the blessed image of good King Harry. I thought that I smelt gold and silver beneath the barley meal. Bring it straight forth, Miller."

Then slowly the Miller arose to his feet, and slowly and unwillingly he untied the mouth of the bag, and slowly thrust his hands into the meal and began fumbling about with his arms buried to the elbows in the barley flour. The others gathered round him, their heads together, looking and wondering what he would bring forth.

So they stood, all with their heads close together, gazing down into the sack. But while he pretended to be searching for the money, the Miller gathered two great handfuls of meal. "Ha," quoth he, "here they are, the beauties." Then, as the others leaned still more forward to see what he had, he suddenly cast the

The·Four·Yeomen·haue·Merry·
Sport·with·a·Stout·Miller:·

meal into their faces, filling their eyes and noses and mouths with the flour, blinding and half choking them. Arthur a Bland was worse off than any, for his mouth was open, agape with wonder of what was to come, so that a great cloud of flour flew down his throat, setting him a-coughing till he could scarcely stand.

Then, while all four stumbled about, roaring with the smart of the meal in their eyeballs, and while they rubbed their eyes till the tears made great channels on their faces through the meal, the Miller seized another handful of flour and another and another, throwing it in their faces, so that even had they had a glimmering of light before they were now as blind as ever a beggar in Nottinghamshire, while their hair and beards and clothes were as white as snow.

Then catching up his great crab staff, the Miller began laying about him as though he were clean gone mad. This way and that skipped the four, like peas on a drumhead, but they could neither see to defend themselves nor to run away. Thwack! thwack! went the Miller's cudgel across their backs, and at every blow great white clouds of flour rose in the air from their jackets and went drifting down the breeze.

"Stop!" roared Robin at last. "Give over, good friend, I am Robin Hood!"

"Thou liest, thou knave," cried the Miller, giving him a rap on the ribs that sent up a great cloud of flour like a puff of smoke, "Stout Robin never robbed an honest tradesman. Ha! thou wouldst have my money, wouldst thou?" And he gave him another blow. "Nay, thou art not getting thy share, thou long-legged knave. Share and share alike." And he smote Little John across the shoulders so that he sent him skipping half across the road. "Nay, fear not, it is thy turn now, black beard." And he gave the Tanner a crack that made him roar for all his coughing. "How now, red coat, let me brush the dust from thee!" cried he, smiting Will Scarlet. And so he gave them merry words and blows until they could scarcely stand, and whenever he saw one like to clear his eyes he threw more flour in his face.

At last Robin Hood found his horn, and clapping it
to his lips blew three loud blasts upon it.

Now it chanced that Will Stutely and a party of
Robin's men were in the glade not far from where
this merry sport was going forward. Hearing the hubbub of voices, and blows that sounded like the noise
of a flail in the barn in winter time, they stopped,
listening, and wondering what was toward. Quoth
Will Stutely, "Now if I mistake not there is some
stout battle with cudgels going forward not far hence.
I would fain see this pretty sight." So saying, he and
the whole party turned their steps whence the noise
came. When they had come near where all the tumult
sounded they heard the three blasts of Robin's bugle
horn.

"Quick!" cried young David of Doncaster. "Our
master is in sore need!" So, without stopping a
moment, they dashed forward with might and main
and burst forth from the covert into the high-road.

But what a sight was that which they saw. The road
was all white with meal, and five men stood there also

white with meal from top to toe, for much of the barley flour had fallen back upon the Miller.

"What is thy need, master?" cried Will Stutely. "And what doth all this mean?"

"Why," quoth Robin in a mighty passion, "yon traitor fellow hath come as nigh slaying me as e'er a man in all the world. Hadst thou not come quickly, good Stutely, thy master had been dead."

Hereupon, whilst he and the three others rubbed the meal from their eyes, and Will Stutely and his men brushed their clothes clean, he told them all; how that he had meant to pass a jest upon the Miller, which same had turned so grievously upon them.

"Quick, men, seize the vile Miller!" cried Stutely, who was nigh choking with laughter as were the rest; whereupon several ran upon the stout fellow, and seizing him bound his arms behind his back with bowstrings.

"Ha!" cried Robin, when they brought the trembling Miller to him. "Thou wouldst murder me, wouldst thou? By my faith"—Here he stopped and stood glaring upon the Miller with a grim look. But Robin's anger could not hold, so first his eyes twinkled, and then in spite of all he broke into a laugh.

Now when they saw their master laugh, the yeomen who stood around could contain themselves no longer, and a mighty shout of laughter went up from all. Many could not stand, but rolled upon the ground from pure merriment.

"What is thy name, good fellow?" said Robin at last to the Miller, who stood gaping and as though he were in a maze.

"Alas, sir, I am Midge, the Miller's son," said he in a frightened voice.

"I make my vow," quoth merry Robin, smiting him upon the shoulder, "thou art the mightiest Midge that e'er mine eyes beheld. Now wilt thou leave thy dusty mill and come and join my band? By my faith, thou art too stout a man to spend thy days betwixt the hopper and the till."

"Then truly, if thou dost forgive me for the blows I struck, not knowing who thou wast, I will join with thee right merrily," said the Miller.

"Then have I gained this day," quoth Robin, "the three stoutest yeomen in all Nottinghamshire. We will get us away to the greenwood tree, and there hold a merry feast in honor of our new friends, though I warrant it will be many a day before I am again the man I was." So saying, he turned and led the way, the rest following, and so they entered the forest once more and were lost to sight.

So that night all was ablaze with crackling fires in the woodlands, for though Robin and those others spoken of, only excepting Midge, the Miller's son, had many a sore bump and bruise here and there on their bodies, they were still not so sore in the joints that they could not enjoy a jolly feast given all in welcome to the new members of the band. Thus with songs and jesting and laughter that echoed through the deeper and more silent nooks of the forest, the night passed quickly along, as such merry times are wont to do, until at last each man sought his couch and silence fell on all things and all things seemed to sleep.

Thus came about three merry adventures in one day, the one stepping upon the heels of another.

But Little John's tongue was ever one that was not easy of guidance, so that, inch by inch, the whole story of his fight with the Tanner and Robin's fight with Will Scarlet leaked out. And so I have told it that you may laugh at the merry tale along with me.

CHAPTER X

How Robin Hood met
Friar Tuck

The stout yeomen of Sherwood Forest were ever early risers of a morn, more especially when the summer time had come, for then in the freshness of the dawn the dew was always the brightest, and the song of the small birds the sweetest.

Quoth Robin, "Now will I go to seek some adventure this merry day."

Then straightway he donned a fine steel coat of chain mail, over which he put on a light jacket of Lincoln green. Upon his head he clapped a steel cap, and this he covered by one of soft white leather, in which stood a nodding cock's plume. By his side he hung a good broadsword of tempered steel, the bluish blade marked all over with strange figures of dragons, winged women, and what not. A gallant sight was Robin so arrayed, I wot, the glint of steel showing here and there as the sunlight caught brightly the links of polished mail that showed beneath his green coat.

So, having arrayed himself, he set forth upon his way, till high noontide was passed, when at last he came to the banks of a wide, glassy, and lily-padded stream. Here a broad beaten path stretched along beside the banks, on which path labored the horses that tugged at the slow moving barges, laden with barley-meal or what not, from the countryside to the many-towered town. At a certain place where this road took a sudden bend Robin stopped suddenly, for he thought that he heard voices. He stood still and listened, and presently heard words passed back and forth betwixt what seemed to be two men, and yet the two voices were wondrously alike. The sound came from over behind the bank, that here was steep and high, dropping from the edge of the road a half a score of feet to the sedgy verge of the river.

" 'Tis strange," muttered Robin to himself after a space, when the voices had ceased their talking; "surely there be two people that spoke the one to the

other, and yet methinks their voices are mightily alike.
I make my vow that never have I heard the like in all
my life before. Truly, if this twain are to be judged by
their voices no two peas were ever more alike. I will
look into this matter.'' So saying, he came softly to the
river bank, and laying him down upon the grass
peered over the edge and down below.

All was cool and shady beneath the bank. A stout
osier grew, not straight upward, but leaning across
the water, shadowing the spot with its soft foliage. All
around grew a mass of feathery ferns such as hide and
nestle in cool places, and up to Robin's nostrils came
the tender odor of the wild thyme, that loves the moist
verges of running streams. Here, with his broad back
against the rugged trunk of the willow tree, and half
hidden by the soft ferns around him, sat a stout,
brawny fellow, but no other man was there. His head
was as round as a ball, and covered with a mat of close-
clipped, curly black hair that grew low down on his
forehead. But his crown was shorn as smooth as the
palm of one's hand, which, together with his loose

robe, cowl, and string of beads, showed that which
his looks never would have done, that he was a Friar.
His cheeks were as red and shining as a winter crab,
albeit they were nearly covered over with a close
curly black beard, as were his chin and upper lip likewise. His neck was thick like that of a north country
bull, and his round head closely set upon shoulders
e'en a match for those of Little John himself. Beneath
his bushy black brows danced a pair of little gray eyes
that could not stand still for very drollery of humor.
No man could look into his face and not feel his heart-
strings tickled by the merriment of their look. By his
side lay a steel cap, which he had laid off for the sake
of coolness to his crown. His legs were stretched wide
apart, and betwixt his knees he held a great pasty
compounded of juicy meats of divers kinds made
savory with tender young onions, both meat and onions
being mingled with a good rich gravy. In his right fist
he held a great piece of brown crust at which he
munched sturdily.

"By my faith," quoth Robin to himself, "I do

The Merry Friar sings a goodly song

verily believe that this is the merriest feast, the merriest wight, the merriest place, and the merriest sight in all merry England. Methought there was another here, but it must have been this holy man talking to himself. Hey friend," cried he aloud, "canst thou tell me how to cross this stream to t'other side?"

No sooner did the holy man hear the unexpected sound of a strange voice than he seized his steel cap, clapped it on his head, and springing to his feet cried in a great voice, "What spy have we here? Come forth, and I will carve thee into as fine pudding-meat as e'er a wife in Yorkshire cooked of a Sunday." Hereupon he drew from beneath his robes a great broadsword full as stout as was Robin's.

"Nay, nay, friend," quoth Robin laughing. "I am no spy, but an honest yeoman in search of adventure who would fain cross this fair stream."

"Truly, friend," quoth the other, mollified by Robin's peaceful words. "Far is it from me to stay thee. Yonder is the ford and the river is free to all."

"Yea, good father," said Robin; "but thou seest

that my clothes are of the finest and I fain would not get them wet. Methinks thy shoulders are stout and broad; couldst thou not find it in thy heart to carry me across?"

"Now, by the white hand of the holy Lady of the Fountain!" burst forth the Friar in a mighty rage; "dost thou, thou poor puny stripling, thou kiss-my-lady-la-poppenjay; thou—thou—What shall I call thee? Dost thou ask me, the holy Tuck, to carry thee? Now I swear"—Here he paused suddenly, then slowly the anger passed from his face, and his little eyes twinkled once more. "But why should I not?" quoth he, piously; "Did not the holy Saint Christopher ever carry the stranger across the river? and should I, poor sinner that I am, be ashamed to do likewise? Come with me, stranger, and I will do thy bidding in an humble frame of mind." So saying he clambered up the bank, and led the way to the shallow pebbly ford, chuckling to himself the while as though he were enjoying some goodly jest within himself.

Having come to the ford, he girded up his robes

about his loins, tucked his good broadsword beneath
his arm, and stooped his back to take Robin upon it.
Suddenly he straightened up. "Methinks," quoth he,
"thou'll get thy weapon wet. Let me tuck it beneath
mine arm along with mine own."

"Nay, good father," said Robin, "I would not
burden thee with aught of mine but myself."

"Dost thou think," said the Friar, mildly, "that
the good Saint Christopher would ha' sought his own
ease so? Nay, give me thy tool as I bid thee, for I
would carry it as a penance to my pride."

Upon this, without more ado, Robin Hood un-
buckled his sword from his side and handed it to the
other, who thrust it with his own beneath his arm.
Then once more the Friar bent his back, and, Robin
having mounted upon it, he stepped sturdily into the
water, and so strode onward, splashing in the shoal,
and breaking all the smooth surface into ever-widening
rings. At last he reached the other side and Robin
leaped lightly from his back.

"Many thanks, good father," quoth he. "Thou art

The·Merry·Friar·carrieth·
Robin·across·the·Water·:·.

indeed a good and holy man. Prythee give me my
sword and let me away, for I am in haste.''

At this the stout Friar looked upon Robin for a long
time, his head on one side, and with a most waggish
twist to his face; then he slowly winked his right eye.
''Nay, good youth,'' said he, gently, ''I doubt not
that thou art in haste with thine affairs, yet thou dost
think nothing of mine. Thine are of a carnal nature;
mine are of a spiritual nature, a holy work, so to speak;
moreover, mine affairs do lie upon the other side of
this stream. I see that thou art a good young man and,
I doubt not, are most reverent to the cloth. I did get
wet coming hither, and am sadly afraid that, should I
wade the water again, I might get certain cricks and
pains i' the joints that would mar my devotions for
many a day to come. I know that since I have so
humbly done thy bidding thou wilt carry me back
again. Thou seest how Saint Godrick, that holy hermit
whose natal day this is, hath placed in my hands two
swords and in thine never a one. Therefore be per-
suaded, good youth, and carry me back again.''

Robin Hood looked up and he looked down, biting his nether lip. Quoth he, "Thou cunning Friar, thou hast me fair and fast enow. Let me tell thee that no one hath so hoodwinked me in all my life before. I might have known from thy looks that thou wert no such holy man as thou didst pretend to be."

"Nay," interrupted the Friar, "I bid thee speak not so scurrilously neither, lest thou mayst perchance feel the prick of an inch or so of blue steel."

"Tut, tut," said Robin, "speak not so, Friar; the loser hath ever the right to use his tongue as he doth list. Give me my sword; I do promise to carry thee back straightway. Nay, I will not lift the weapon against thee."

"Marry, come up," quoth the Friar, "I fear thee not, fellow. Here is thy skewer; and get thyself presently ready, for I would hasten back."

So Robin took his sword again and buckled it at his side; then he bent his stout back and took the Friar upon it.

Now I wot Robin Hood had a heavier load to carry

in the Friar than the Friar had in him. Moreover he did not know the ford, so he went stumbling among the stones, now stepping into a deep hole, and now nearly tripping over a bowlder, while the sweat ran down his face in beads from the hardness of his journey and the heaviness of his load. Meantime, the Friar kept digging his heels into Robin's sides and bidding him hasten, calling him many ill names the while. To all this Robin answered never a word, but, having softly felt around till he found the buckle of the belt that held the Friar's sword, he worked slyly at the fastenings, seeking to loosen them. Thus it came about that, by the time he had reached the other bank with his load, the Friar's swordbelt was loose albeit he knew it not; so when Robin stood on dry land and the Friar leaped from his back, the yeoman gripped hold of the sword so that blade, sheath, and strap came away from the holy man, leaving him without a weapon.

"Now, then," quoth merry Robin, panting as he spake and wiping the sweat from his brow, "I have thee, fellow. This time that same Saint of whom thou didst speak but now hath delivered two swords into my hand and hath stripped thine away from thee. Now if thou dost not carry me back, and that speedily, I swear I will prick thy skin till it is as full of holes as a slashed doublet.''

The good Friar said not a word for a while, but he looked at Robin with a grim look. ''Now,'' said he at last, ''I did think that thy wits were of the heavy sort and knew not that thou wert so cunning. Truly, thou hast me upon the hip. Give me my sword, and I promise not to draw it against thee save in self-defense; also I promise to do thy bidding and take thee upon my back and carry thee.''

So jolly Robin gave him his sword again, which the Friar buckled to his side, and this time looked to it that it was more secure in its fastenings; then tucking up his robes once more, he took Robin Hood upon his back and without a word stepped into the water, and so waded on in silence while Robin sat laughing upon his back. At last they reached the middle of the ford where the water was deepest. Here the Friar stopped

for a moment, and then, with a sudden lift of his hand
and heave of his shoulders, fairly shot Robin over his
head as though he were a sack of grain.

Down went Robin into the water with a mighty
splash. "There," quoth the holy man, calmly turning
back again to the shore, "let that cool thy hot spirit,
if it may."

Meantime, after much splashing, Robin had got to
his feet and stood gazing about him all bewildered, the
water running from him in pretty little rills. At last
he shot the water out of his ears and spat some out of
his mouth, and, gathering his scattered wits together,
saw the stout Friar standing on the bank and laughing.
Then, I wot, was Robin Hood a mad man. "Stay, thou
villain!" roared he, "I am after thee straight, and if I
do not carve thy brawn for thee this day, may I never
lift finger again!" So saying, he dashed, splashing, to
the bank.

"Thou needest not hasten thyself unduly," quoth
the stout Friar. "Fear not; I will abide here, and if
thou dost not cry 'Alack-a-day' ere long time is gone,

may I never more peep through the brake at a fallow
deer."

And now Robin, having reached the bank, began,
without more ado, to roll up his sleeves above his
wrists. The Friar, also, tucked his robes more about
him, showing a great, stout arm on which the muscles
stood out like humps of an aged tree. Then Robin saw,
what he had not wotted of before, that the Friar had
also a coat of chain mail beneath his gown.

"Look to thyself," cried Robin, drawing his good
sword.

"Ay, marry," quoth the Friar, who held his already
in his hand. So, without more ado, they came together, and thereupon began a fierce and mighty
battle. Right and left, and up and down, and back and
forth they fought. The swords flashed in the sun and
then met with a clash that sounded far and near. I wot
this was no playful bout at quarterstaff, but a grim and
serious fight of real earnest. Thus they strove for an
hour or more, pausing every now and then to rest, at
which times each looked at the other with wonder,

and thought that never had he seen so stout a fellow;
then once again they would go at it more fiercely than
ever. Yet in all this time neither had harmed the other
nor caused his blood to flow. At last merry Robin
cried, "Hold thy hand, good friend!" whereupon
both lowered their swords.

"Now," quoth Robin, wiping the sweat from his
brow, "thou art the fairest swordsman I have fallen
in with for many a long day. What may be thy name, I
prythee, good and reverend father?"

"Why, truly," said the Friar, demurely, "some do
call me the curtal Friar of Fountain Dale; others again
call me in jest the Abbot of Fountain Abbey; others
still again call me simple Friar Tuck."

"I like the last name best," quoth Robin, "for it
doth slip more glibly off the tongue. Mine own name,
I may tell thee, is Robin Hood."

"Robin Hood!" cried the other. "Robin Hood!
Art thou, indeed, that famous yeoman?"

"Ay," quoth merry Robin, "that man am I and
none other. And now, good father, we have need in

the greenwood of just such an holy man as thou art to advise us from evil ways. Wilt thou leave thine hermitage and come with me to Sherwood to join my goodly band?"

"Indeed will I," cried the other, "and that right gladly, for such a life fitteth mine inclinations as the haft fitteth to the blade."

CHAPTER XI

How Robin Hood shot before Queen Eleanor

And now the fame of Robin Hood had spread far and wide, until at last it reached even to the ears of good Queen Eleanor in famous London Town. "Fain would I see this bold yeoman," quoth she, "and fain would I behold his skill with the longbow of which we have heard so much."

Under the greenwood tree, in the cool shade that spread all around upon the sward, with flickering lights here and there, Robin Hood and many of his band lay upon the soft green grass, whilst Allan a Dale, the sweet-singing minstrel of the band, sang and played upon his harp. All listened in silence, for young Allan's singing was one of the greatest joys in all the world to them. But as they so listened there came of a sudden a sound of horse's feet, and presently Little John and Will Stutely came forth from the forest path into the open glade, a beautiful young Page, gay with crimson and gold, riding between them upon a milk-white horse. The three came toward where Robin Hood sat, all the band staring with might and main, for never had they seen so gay a sight as this young Page, nor one so richly clad in silks and velvets and gold and jewels. Then Robin Hood arose and stepped forth to meet him, and the other leaped from his horse, and doffing his cap of crimson velvet, met Robin as he came.

"Now, welcome!" cried Robin. "Now, welcome, fair youth; and tell me, I prythee, what bringeth one of so fair a presence and clad in such noble garb to our poor forest of Sherwood?"

Then the youth said: "If I err not, thou art the

famous Robin Hood, and these thy stout band of outlawed yeomen. I am Richard Partington and Page to
Her Royal Majesty. To thee I bring greeting from our
noble Queen Eleanor. Oft hath she heard thee spoken
of and thy merry doings hereabouts, and fain would
she behold thy face; therefore she bids me tell thee
that if thou wilt presently come to London Town, she
will do all in her power to guard thee against harm,
and will send thee back safe to Sherwood Forest again.
Four days hence, in Finsbury Fields, our good King
Henry, of great renown, holdeth a grand shooting-
match, and all the most famous archers of merry
England will be thereat. Our Queen would fain see
thee strive with these, knowing that if thou wilt come
thou wilt, with little doubt, carry off the prize. Therefore she hath sent me with this greeting, and furthermore sends thee, as a sign of great good will, this
golden ring from off her own fair thumb, which I give
herewith into thy hands.''

Then Robin Hood bowed his head, and taking the
ring kissed it right loyally, and then slipped it upon his

little finger. Quoth he, "Sooner would I lose my life than this ring; and ere it departs from me, my hand shall be cold in death or stricken off at the wrist. Fair Sir Page, I will do our Queen's bidding, and will presently hie with thee to London; but, ere we go, I will feast thee here in the woodlands with the very best we have."

"It may not be," said the Page; "we have no time to tarry, therefore get thyself ready straightway; and if there be any of thy band that thou wouldst take with thee, our Queen bids me say that she will make them right welcome likewise."

"As thou sayst," quoth Robin, "so it shall be; therefore I will get me ready presently. I will choose three of my men, only, to go with me, and these three shall be Little John, mine own true right-hand man, Will Scarlet, my cousin, and Allan a Dale, my minstrel. Go, lads, and get ye ready straightway, and we will presently off with all speed that we may. Thou, Will Stutely, shall be the chief of the band while I am gone."

Then Little John and Will Scarlet and Allan a Dale

ran leaping, full of joy, to make themselves ready,
whilst Robin also prepared himself for the journey.
After a while they all four came forth, and a right fair
sight they made, for Robin was clad in blue from head
to foot, and Little John and Will Scarlet in good
Lincoln green, and as for Allan a Dale, he was dressed
in scarlet from the crown of his head to the toes of his
pointed shoes. Each man wore beneath his cap a little
head-covering of burnished steel set with rivets of
gold, and underneath his jerkin a coat of linked mail,
as fine as carded wool, yet so tough that no arrow
could pierce it. Then, seeing all were ready, young
Partington mounted his horse again, and the yeomen
having shaken hands all around, the five departed upon
their way.

Queen Eleanor sat in her royal bower, through the
open casements of which poured the sweet yellow
sunshine in great floods of golden light. All about her
stood her ladies in waiting chatting in low voices,
whilst she herself sat dreamily where the mild air

came softly drifting into the room laden with the fresh perfumes of the sweet red roses that bloomed in the great garden beneath the wall. To her came one who said that her page, Richard Partington, and four stout yeomen, waited her pleasure in the court below. Then Queen Eleanor arose joyously and bade them be straightway shown into her presence.

Thus Robin Hood and Little John and Will Scarlet and Allan a Dale came before the Queen into her own royal bower. Then Robin kneeled before the Queen with his hands folded upon his breast, saying, in simple phrase, "Here am I, Robin Hood. Thou didst bid me come, and lo, I do thy bidding. I give myself to thee as thy true servant, and will do thy commanding, even if it be to the shedding of the last drop of my life's blood."

But good Queen Eleanor smiled pleasantly upon him, bidding him to arise; then she made them all be seated to rest themselves after their long journey. Rich food was brought them and noble wines, and she had her own pages to wait upon the wants of the yeo-

men. At last, after they had eaten all they could, she
began questioning them of their merry adventures.
Then they told her all of the lusty doings herein spoken
of, and the Queen and the ladies about her laughed
again and again at the joyous stories. Then, when they
had told all that they could bring to mind, the Queen
asked Allan to sing to her, for his fame as a minstrel
had reached even to the court at London Town, and
Allan did as he was bidden, and the Queen and her
ladies listened in silence.

A gay sight were famous Finsbury Fields on that
bright and sunny morning of lusty summertime. Along
the end of the meadow stood the booths for the different bands of archers, for the King's yeomen were
divided into companies of fourscore men, and each
company had a captain over it; so on the bright green-
sward stood ten booths of striped canvas, a booth for
each band of the royal archers, and at the peak of each
fluttered a flag in the mellow air, and the flag was the
color that belonged to the captain of each band. From

ALLAN·A·DALE·SINGETH·BE-
FORE·OVR·GOOD·QVEEN·EL=
EANOR·   ·MDCCCXXCIII·

the centre booth hung the yellow flag of **Tepus,** the
famous bow-bearer of the King; next to it, on one
hand, was the blue flag of Gilbert of the White Hand,
and on the other the blood-red pennant of stout young
Clifton of Buckinghamshire. The seven other archer
captains were also men of great renown; among them
were Egbert of Kent and William of Southampton;
but those first named were most famous of all. The
noise of many voices in talk and laughter came from
within the booths, and in and out ran the attendants
like ants about an ant hill. On each side of the archery
range were rows upon rows of seats reaching high
aloft, and in the centre of the north side was a raised
dais for the King and Queen, shaded by canvas of gay
colors, and hung about with streaming silken pennants
of red and blue and green and white. As yet the King
and Queen had not come, but all the other benches
were full of people, rising head above head high aloft
till it made the eye dizzy to look upon them. Eightscore yards distant from the mark from which the
archers were to shoot stood ten fair targets, each

target marked by a flag of the color belonging to the
band that was to shoot thereat. So all was ready and all
waited for the coming of the King and Queen.

At last a great blast of bugles sounded, and into the
meadow came riding six trumpeters, with silver
trumpets, from which hung velvet banners heavy with
rich workings of silver and gold thread. Behind these
came stout King Henry upon a dapple-gray stallion,
with his Queen beside him upon a milk-white palfrey.
On either side of them walked the yeomen of the
guard, the bright sunlight flashing from the polished
blades of the steel halberds they carried. Behind these
came the Court in a great crowd, so that presently all
the lawn was alive with bright colors, with silk and
velvet, with waving plumes and gleaming gold, with
flashing jewels and sword hilts; a gallant sight on that
bright summer day.

Then all the people arose and shouted, so that their
voices sounded like the storm upon the Cornish coast,
when the dark waves run upon the shore and leap and
break, surging amid the rocks; so, amid the roaring

and the surging of the people, and the waving of
scarfs and kerchiefs, the King and Queen came to
their place, and, getting down from their horses,
mounted the broad stairs that led to the raised platform, and there took their seats on two thrones bedecked with purple silks and cloths of silver and of
gold.

When all was quiet a bugle sounded, and straightway the archers came marching in order from their
tents. Fortyscore they were in all, as stalwart a band
of yeomen as could be found in all the wide world.
So they came in orderly fashion and stood in front of
the dais where King Henry and his Queen sat. King
Henry looked up and down their ranks right proudly,
for his heart warmed within him at the sight of such a
gallant band of yeomen. Then he bade his herald, Sir
Hugh de Mowbray, stand forth and proclaim the rules
governing the game. So Sir Hugh stepped to the edge
of the platform and spoke in a loud clear voice, so
that they could hear him even to the ends of the range,
and thus he said:—

That each man should shoot seven arrows at the target that belonged to his band, and, of the fourscore yeomen of each band, the three that shot the best should be chosen. These three should shoot three arrows apiece, and the one that shot the best should again be chosen. Then each of these should again shoot three arrows apiece, and the one that shot the best should have the first prize, the one that shot the next best should have the second, and the one that shot the next best should have the third prize. Each of the others should have fourscore silver pennies for his shooting. The first prize was to be twoscore and ten golden pounds, a silver bugle horn inlaid with gold, and a quiver with ten white arrows tipped with gold and feathered with white swan's wing therein. The second prize was to be fivescore of the fattest bucks that run on Dallen Lea, to be shot when the yeoman that won them chose. The third prize was to be two tuns of good Rhenish wine.

So Sir Hugh spoke, and when he had done all the archers waved their bows aloft and shouted. Then each band turned and marched in order back to its place.

And now the shooting began, the captains first taking stand and speeding their shafts and then making room for the men who shot, each in turn after them. Two hundred and eightyscore shafts were shot in all, and so deftly were they sped that when the shooting was done each target looked like the back of a hedgehog when the farm dog snuffs at it. A long time was taken in this shooting, and when it was over the judges came forward, looked carefully at the targets, and proclaimed in a loud voice which three had shot the best from the separate bands. Then a great hubbub of voices arose, each man among the crowd that looked on calling for his favorite archer. Then ten fresh targets were brought forward, and every sound was hushed as the archers took their places once more.

This time the shooting was more speedily done, for only nine shafts were shot by each band. Not an arrow missed the targets, but in that of Gilbert of the White Hand five arrows were in the small white spot that

marked the centre; of these five three were sped by
Gilbert. Then the judges came forward again, and
looking at the targets, called aloud the names of the
archer chosen as the best bowman of each band. Of
these Gilbert of the White Hand led, for six of the ten
arrows he had shot had lodged in the centre; but stout
Tepus and young Clifton trod close upon his heels;
yet the others stood a fair chance for the second or
third place.

And now, amid the roaring of the crowd, those ten
stout fellows that were left went back to their tents to
rest for a while and change their bowstrings, for
naught must fail at this next round, and no hand must
tremble or eye grow dim because of weariness.

Then whilst the deep buzz and hum of talking
sounded all around like the noise of the wind in the
leafy forest, Queen Eleanor turned to the King, and
quoth she, "Thinkest thou that these young yeomen
so chosen are the very best archers in all merry
England?"

"Yea, truly," said the King, smiling, for he was

well pleased with the sport that he had seen; "and I tell thee, that not only are they the best archers in all merry England, but in all the wide world beside."

"But what wouldst thou say," quoth Queen Eleanor, "if I were to find three archers to match the best three yeomen of all thy guard?"

"I would say thou hast done what I could not do," said the King, laughing, "for I tell thee there lives not in all the world three archers to match Tepus and Gilbert and Clifton of Buckinghamshire."

"Now," said the Queen, "I know of three yeomen, and in truth I have seen them not long since, that I would not fear to match against any three that thou canst choose from among all thy fortyscore archers; and, moreover, I will match them here this very day. But I will only match them with thy archers providing that thou wilt grant a free pardon to all that may come in my behalf."

At this the King laughed loud and long. "Truly," said he, "thou art taking up with strange matters for a queen. If thou wilt bring those three fellows that thou

speakest of I will promise faithfully to give them free
pardon for forty days, to come or go wheresoever they
please, nor will I harm a hair of their heads in all that
time. Moreover, if these that thou bringest shoot better
than my yeomen, man for man, they shall have the
prizes for themselves according to their shooting. But
as thou hast so taken up of a sudden with sports of this
kind, hast thou a mind for a wager?"

"Why, in sooth," said Queen Eleanor, laughing,
"I know naught of such matters, but if thou hast a
mind to do somewhat in that way, I will strive to
pleasure thee. What wilt thou wager upon thy men?"

Then the merry King laughed again, for he dearly
loved a goodly jest; so he said, amidst his laughter, "I
will wager thee ten tuns of Rhenish wine, ten tuns of
the stoutest ale, and tenscore bows of tempered
Spanish yew, with quivers and arrows to match."

All that stood around smiled at this, for it seemed a
merry wager for a king to give to a queen, but Queen
Eleanor bowed her head quietly. "I will take thy
wager," said she, "for I know right well where to

place those things that thou hast spoken of. Now, who
will be on my side in this matter?'' And she looked
around upon them that stood about; but no one spake
or cared to wager upon the Queen's side against such
archers as Tepus and Gilbert and Clifton. Then the
Queen spoke again: ''Now, who will back me in this
wager?''

And then as no one ventured she said, ''Nay, I need
no man's aid in this undertaking; but against thy wine
and beer and stout bows of yew I wager this girdle all
set with jewels from around my waist; and surely that
is worth more than thine.''

''Now, I take thy wager,'' quoth the King. ''Send
for thy archers straightway. But here come forth the
others; let them shoot, and then I will match those
that win against all the world.''

''So be it,'' said the Queen. Thereupon, beckoning
to young Richard Partington, she whispered something in his ear, and straightway the Page bowed and
left the place, crossing the meadow to the other side
of the range, where he was presently lost in the crowd.
At this all that stood around whispered to one another,

wondering what it all meant, and what three men the
Queen was about to set against those famous archers
of the King's guard.

And now the ten archers of the King's guard took
their stand again, and all the great crowd was hushed
to the stillness of death. Slowly and carefully each man
shot his shafts, and so deep was the silence that you
could hear every arrow rap against the target as it
struck it. Then, when the last shaft had sped, a great
roar went up; and the shooting, I wot, was well
worthy of the sound. Once again Gilbert had lodged
three arrows in the white; Tepus came second with
two in the white and one in the black ring next to it;
but stout Clifton had gone down and Hubert of
Suffolk had taken the third place, for, while both
those two good yeomen had lodged two in the white,
Clifton had lost one shot upon the fourth ring, and
Hubert came in with one in the third.

All the archers around Gilbert's booth shouted for
joy till their throats were hoarse, tossing their caps
aloft, and shaking hands with one another.

In the midst of all this noise and hubbub five men

came walking across the lawn toward the King's
pavilion. The first was Richard Partington, and was
known to most folk there, but the others were strange
to everybody. Beside young Partington walked a yeoman clad in blue, and behind came three others, two
in Lincoln green and one in scarlet. This last yeoman
carried three stout bows of yew tree, two fancifully
inlaid with silver and one with gold. Whilst these five
men came walking across the meadow, a messenger
came running from the King's booth, and summoned
Gilbert and Tepus and Hubert to go with him. And
now the shouting quickly ceased, for all saw that something unwonted was toward, so the folk stood up in
their places and leaned forward to see what was
the ado.

When Partington and the others came before the
spot where the King and Queen sat, the four yeoman
bent their knees and doffed their caps unto her.

Then the Queen leaned forward and spake in a clear
voice, "Locksley," said she, "I have laid a wager with
the King that thou and two of thy men can outshoot

any three that he can send against you. Will thou do
thy best for my sake?"

The King turned to the Queen, and quoth he,
"Who are these men that thou hast brought before
us?"

Now it happened that in the company then present
was the Sheriff of Nottingham. When he beheld the
four yeomen his face turned as pale as wax and then as
red as a cherry. Then straighway up he spake, thinking naught either of King or Queen: "Your majesty,"
quoth he, "yon fellow in blue is a certain outlawed
thief of the midcountry, named Robin Hood; yon tall,
strapping villain goeth by the name of Little John; the
other fellow in green is a certain backsliding gentle-
man, known as Will Scarlet; the man in red is a rogue
of a northern minstrel, named Allan a Dale."

At this speech the King's brows drew together
blackly, and he turned to the Queen. "Is this true?"
said he, sternly.

"Yea," said the Queen, smiling, "the Sheriff
should know them well, and he hath told the truth;

but bear in mind that thou hast pledged thy promise
for the safety of these good yeomen for forty days.''

"I will keep my promise," said the King, in a deep
voice that showed the anger in his heart; "but when
these forty days are gone let this outlaw look to himself, for mayhap things will not go so smoothly with
him as he would like." Then he turned to his archers,
who stood near the Sherwood yeomen, listening and
wondering at all that passed. Quoth he, "Gilbert, and
thou, Tepus, and thou, Hubert, I have pledged myself
that ye shall shoot against these three fellows. If ye
outshoot the knaves I will fill your caps with silver
pennies; if ye fail ye shall lose your prizes that ye have
won so fairly, and they go to them that shoot against
you, man to man. Do your best, lads, and if ye win
this bout ye shall be glad of it to the last days of your
life. Go, now, and get you gone to the butts."

Then the three archers of the King turned and went
back to their booths, and Robin and his men went to
their places at the mark from which they were to
shoot. Then they strung their bows and made them-

The·Sheriff·of·Nottingham·cometh·
before·the·King·at·London

selves ready, looking over their quivers of arrows, and picking out the roundest and the best feathered.

Six fresh targets were now set up, one for each man that was to shoot; whereupon Gilbert and Tepus and Hubert came straightway forth from the booths. Then Robin Hood and Gilbert of the White Hand tossed a farthing aloft to see who should lead in the shooting, and the lot fell to Gilbert's side; thereupon he called upon Hubert of Suffolk to lead.

Hubert took his place, planted his foot firmly, and fitted a fair, smooth arrow; then, breathing upon his finger-tips, he drew the string slowly and carefully. The arrow sped true, and lodged in the white; again he shot, and again he hit the clout; a third shaft he sped, but this time failed of the centre, and but struck the black, yet not more than a finger's breadth from the white. At this a shout went up, for it was the best shooting that Hubert had yet done that day.

Merry Robin laughed, and quoth he, "Thou wilt have an ill time bettering that round, Will, for it is thy turn next. Brace thy thews, lad, and bring not shame upon Sherwood."

Then Will Scarlet took his place; but, because of
over-caution, he spoiled his target with the very first
arrow that he sped, for he hit the next ring to the
black, the second from the centre. At this Robin bit
his lips. "Lad, lad," quoth he, "hold not the string
so long! Have I not often told thee what Gaffer Swanthold sayeth, that 'overcaution spilleth the milk?'"
To this Will Scarlet took heed, so the next arrow he
shot lodged fairly in the centre ring; again he shot, and
again he smote the centre; but, for all that, stout
Hubert had outshot him, and showed the better target. Then all those that looked on clapped their hands
for joy because that Hubert had overcome the stranger.

Quoth the King, grimly, to the Queen, "If thy
archers shoot no better than that, thou art like to lose
thy wager, lady." But Queen Eleanor smiled, for she
looked for better things from Robin Hood and Little
John.

And now Tepus took his place to shoot. He, also,
took over-heed to what he was about, and so he fell
into Will Scarlet's error. The first arrow he struck

into the centre ring, but the second missed its mark,
and smote the black; the last arrow was tipped with
luck, for it smote the very centre of the clout, upon
the black spot that marked it. Quoth Robin Hood,
"That is the sweetest shot that hath been sped this
day; but, nevertheless, friend Tepus, thy cake is
burned, methinks. Little John, it is thy turn next."

So Little John took his place as bidden, and shot his
three arrows quickly. He never lowered his bow arm
in all the shooting, but fitted each shaft with his longbow raised; yet all three of his arrows smote the
centre within easy distance of the black. At this no
sound of shouting was heard, for, although it was the
best shooting that had been done that day, the folk of
London Town did not like to see the stout Tepus overcome by a fellow from the countryside, even were he
as famous as Little John.

And now stout Gilbert of the White Hand took his
place and shot with the greatest care; and again, for
the third time in one day, he struck all three shafts
into the clout.

"Well done, Gilbert!" quoth Robin Hood, smiting him upon the shoulder. "I make my vow, thou art one of the best archers that ever mine eyes beheld. Thou shouldst be a free and merry ranger like us, lad, for thou art better fitted for the greenwood than for the cobblestones and gray walls of London Town." So saying, he took his place, and drew a fair, round arrow from his quiver, which he turned over and over ere he fitted it to his bowstring.

Then the King muttered in his beard, "Now, blessed Saint Hubert, if thou wilt but jog that rogue's elbow so as to make him smite even the second ring, I will give eightscore waxen candles three fingers' breadth in thickness to thy chapel nigh Matching." But it may be Saint Hubert's ears were stuffed with tow, for he seemed not to hear the King's prayer this day.

Having gotten three shafts to his liking, merry Robin looked carefully to his bowstring ere he shot. "Yea," quoth he to Gilbert, who stood nigh him to watch his shooting, "thou shouldst pay us a visit at merry Sherwood." Here he drew the bowstring to his ear. "In London"—here he loosed his shaft—"thou canst find naught to shoot at but rooks and daws; there one can tickle the ribs of the noblest stags in England." So he shot even whilst he talked, yet the shaft lodged not more than half an inch from the very centre.

"By my soul!" cried Gilbert. "Art thou the devil in blue, to shoot in that wise?"

"Nay," quoth Robin, laughing, "not quite so ill as that, I trust." And he took up another shaft and fitted it to the string. Again he shot, and again he smote his arrow close beside the centre; a third time he loosed his bowstring, and dropped his arrow just betwixt the other two and into the very centre, so that the feathers of all three were roffled together, seeming from a distance to be one thick shaft.

And now a low murmur ran all among that great crowd, for never before had London seen such shooting as this; and never again would it see it after Robin Hood's day had gone. All saw that the King's archers were fairly beaten, and stout Gilbert clapped his palm to Robin's, owning that he could never hope to draw such a bowstring as Robin Hood or Little John. But the King, full of wrath, would not have it so, though he knew in his mind that his men could not stand against those fellows. "Nay!" cried he, clenching his hands upon the arms of his seat, "Gilbert is not yet beaten! Did he not strike the clout thrice? Although I have lost my wager, he hath not yet lost the first prize. They shall shoot again, and still again, till either he or that knave Robin Hood cometh off the best. Go thou, Sir Hugh, and bid them shoot another round, and another, until one or the other is overcome." Then Sir Hugh, seeing how wroth the King was, said never a word, but went straightway to do his bidding; so he came to where Robin Hood and the other stood, and told them what the King had said.

"With all my heart," quoth merry Robin, "I will shoot from this time till to-morrow day if it can pleasure my most gracious lord and king. Take thy place, Gilbert lad, and shoot."

So Gilbert took his place once more, but this time he failed, for, a sudden little wind arising, his shaft missed the centre ring, but by not more than the breadth of a barley straw.

"Thy eggs are cracked, Gilbert," quoth Robin, laughing; and straightway he loosed a shaft, and once more smote the white circle of the centre.

Then the King arose from his place, and not a word said he, but he looked around with a baleful look, and it would have been an ill day for any one that he saw with a joyous or a merry look upon his face. Then he and his Queen and all the court left the place, but the King's heart was brimming full of wrath within him.

After the King had gone, all the yeomen of the archer guard came crowding around Robin, and Little John, and Will, and Allan, to snatch a look at these famous fellows from the midcountry; and with them came many that had been onlookers at the sport, for the same purpose. Thus it happened presently that the yeomen, to whom Gilbert stood talking, were all surrounded by a crowd of people that formed a ring about them. "Marry," quoth Little John to Will Scarlet, "one would think that these poor fellows had never seen a stout yeoman ranger in all their lives before, or that we were some curious spectacle, like the Cumberland Giant, or the Welsh Dwarf, that we saw last month at the fair at Norwich.''

After a while the three judges that had the giving away of the prizes came forward, and the chief of them all spake to Robin and said: ''According to agreement, the first prize belongeth rightly to thee; so here I give thee the silver bugle, here the quiver of ten golden arrows, and here a purse of twoscore and ten golden pounds.'' And as he spake he handed those things to Robin, and then turned to Little John. ''To thee,'' he said, ''belongeth the second prize, to wit, fivescore of the finest harts that run on Dallen Lea. Thou mayest shoot them whensoever thou dost list.'' Last of all he turned to stout Hubert. ''Thou,'' said he, ''hast held thine own against the yeoman with whom thou didst shoot, and so thou has kept the prize duly thine, to wit, two tuns of good Rhenish wine. These shall be delivered to thee whensoever thou dost list.'' Then he called upon the other seven of the King's archers who had last shot, and gave them each fourscore silver pennies.

Then up spake Robin, and quoth he, "This silver bugle I keep in honor of this shooting-match; but thou, Gilbert, art the best archer of all the King's guard, and to thee I freely give this purse of gold. Take it, man, and would it were ten times as much, for thou art a right yeoman, good and true. Furthermore, to each of the ten that last shot I give one of these golden shafts apiece. Keep them always by you, so that ye may tell your grandchildren, and ye are ever blessed with them, that ye are the very stoutest yeomen in all the wide world."

At this all shouted aloud, for it pleased them to hear Robin speak so of them.

Then up spake Little John. "Good friend Tepus," said he, "I want not those harts of Dallen Lea that yon stout judge spoke of but now, for in truth we have enow and more than enow in our own country. Two-score and ten I give thee for thine own shooting, and five I give to each band for their pleasure."

At this another great shout went up, and many tossed their caps aloft, and swore among themselves that no better fellows ever walked the sod than Robin Hood and his stout yeomen.

Thus ended the famous shooting-match before Queen Eleanor.

And next I will tell you of how Robin Hood met with King Richard of the Lion's Heart in Sherwood Forest. So listen and ye shall hear.

CHAPTER XII

How King Richard came to Sherwood Forest

And now many years had passed. King Henry had died and King Richard of the Lion's Heart had come to the Throne through many adventures as stirring as any that had befallen Robin himself. And now all Nottingham-shire was in a mighty stir and tumult, for King Richard was making a royal progress through merry England, and every one expected him to come to Nottingham Town in his journeying.

So all was bustle and hubbub; a great running hither and thither, a rapping of hammers and a babel of voices sounding everywhere through the place, for the folk were building great arches across the streets, beneath which the King was to pass, and were draping these arches with silken banners and streamers of many colors. Great noise and tumult was going on in the Guild Hall of the town, also, for here a grand banquet was to be given to the King and the nobles of his train, and the best master carpenters were busy building a throne where the King and the Sheriff were to sit at the head of the table, side by side.

Bright shone the sun down into the stony streets, which were all alive with a restless sea of people. On either side of the way great crowds of town and country folks stood packed as close together as dried herring in a box, so that the Sheriff's men, halberds in hands, could hardly press them back to leave space for the King's riding.

"Take care whom thou pushest against!" cried a great, burly friar to one of these men. "Wouldst thou dig thine elbows into me, sirrah? By'r Lady of the Fountain, and thou dost not treat me with more deference I will crack thy knave's pate for thee, even though thou be one of the mighty Sheriff's men."

At this a great shout of laughter arose from a number of tall yeomen in Lincoln green that were scattered through the crowd thereabouts; but one that seemed of more authority than the others nudged the holy man with his elbow, "Peace, Tuck," said he; "didst thou not promise me, ere thou camest here, that thou wouldst put a check upon thy tongue?"

"Ay, marry," grumbled the other, "but a did not think to have a hard-footed knave trample all over my poor toes as though they were no more than so many acorns in the forest."

But of a sudden all this bickering ceased, for a clear sound of many bugle horns came winding down the street. Then all the people craned their necks and gazed in the direction whence the sound came, and the crowding and pushing and the swaying grew greater than ever. And now a gallant array of men came gleaming into sight, and the cheering of the people ran down the crowd as the fire runs in dry grass.

Eight and twenty heralds in velvet and cloth of gold came riding forward. Over their heads fluttered a cloud of snow-white feathers, and each herald bore in his hand a long silver trumpet, which he blew musically. From each trumpet hung a heavy banner of velvet and cloth of gold, with the royal arms of England em-

blazoned thereon. After these came riding fivescore
noble knights, two by two, all fully armed, saving that
their heads were uncovered. In their hands they bore
tall lances, from the tops of which fluttered pennons of
many colors and devices. By the side of each knight
walked a page clad in rich clothes of silk and velvet,
and each page bore in his hands his master's helmet,
from which waved long, floating plumes of feathers.
Never had Nottingham seen a fairer sight than those
fivescore noble knights, from whose armor the sun
blazed in dazzling light as they came riding on their
great war-horses, with clashing of arms and jingling of
chains. Behind the knights came the barons and the
nobles of the midcountry, in robes of silk and cloth of
gold, with golden chains about their necks and jewels
at their girdles. Behind these again came a great array
of men-at-arms, with spears and halberds in their
hands, and, in the midst of these, two riders side by
side. One of the horsemen was the Sheriff of Nottingham in his robes of office. The other, who was a head
taller than the Sheriff, was clad in a rich but simple

garb, with a broad, heavy chain about his neck. His hair and beard were like threads of gold, and his eyes were as blue as the summer sky. As he rode along he bowed to the right hand and the left, and a mighty roar of voices followed him as he passed; for this was King Richard.

Then, above all the tumult and the shouting a great voice was heard roaring, "Heaven, its saints bless thee, our gracious King Richard! and likewise Our Lady of the Fountain, bless thee!" Then King Richard, looking toward the spot whence the sound came, saw a tall, burly, strapping priest standing in front of all the crowd with his legs wide apart as he backed against those behind.

"By my soul, Sheriff," said the King, laughing, "ye have the tallest priests in Nottinghamshire that e'er I saw in all my life. If Heaven never answered prayers because of deafness, methinks I would nevertheless have blessings bestowed upon me, for that man yonder would make the great stone image of Saint Peter rub its ears and hearken unto him. I would that I had an army of such as he."

To this the Sheriff answered never a word, but all the blood left his cheeks, and he caught at the pommel of his saddle to keep himself from falling; for he also saw the fellow that so shouted, and knew him to be Friar Tuck; and moreover, behind Friar Tuck he saw the faces of Robin Hood and Little John and Will Scarlet and Will Stutely and Allan a Dale and others of the band.

"How, now," said the King hastily, "art thou ill, Sheriff, that thou growest so white?"

"Nay, your majesty," said the Sheriff, "it was naught but a sudden pain that will soon pass by." Thus he spake, for he was ashamed that the King should know that Robin Hood feared him so little that he thus dared to come within the very gates of Nottingham Town.

Thus rode the King into Nottingham Town on that bright afternoon in the early fall season; and none rejoiced more than Robin Hood and his merry men to see him come so royally unto his own.

Eventide had come; the great feast in the Guild Hall at Nottingham Town was done. A thousand waxen

lights gleamed along the board, at which sat lord and
noble and knight and squire in goodly array. At the
head of the table, upon a throne all hung with cloth of
gold, sat King Richard with the Sheriff of Nottingham
beside him.

Quoth the King to the Sheriff, laughing as he
spoke, "I have heard much spoken concerning the
doings of certain fellows hereabouts, one Robin Hood
and his band, who are outlaws and abide in Sherwood
Forest. Canst thou not tell me somewhat of them, Sir
Sheriff? for I hear that thou hast had dealings with them
more than once."

At these words the Sheriff of Nottingham looked
down gloomily, gnawing his nether lip. Quoth he, "I
can tell your majesty but little concerning the doings
of those naughty fellows, saving that they are the bold-
est lawbreakers in all the land."

Then up spake young Sir Henry of the Lea, a
great favorite with the King, under whom he had
fought in Palestine, and whose father had once been
helped in time of need by merry Robin. "May it

please your majesty," said he, "when I was away in Palestine I heard ofttimes from my father, and in most cases I heard of this very fellow, Robin Hood. If your majesty would like I will tell you a certain adventure of this outlaw."

Then the King laughingly bade him tell his tale, whereupon he told how the Sheriff had tried to buy the horned beasts of Robin Hood, and how he had paid so dear a price for a merry feast in the greenwood. Again and again the King and those present roared with laughter, whilst the poor Sheriff waxed cherry red in the face with vexation, for the matter was a sore thing with him. When Sir Henry of the Lea was done, others of those present, seeing how the King enjoyed this merry tale, told other tales concerning Robin and his merry men.

"By the hilt of my sword," said stout King Richard, "this is as bold and merry a knave as ever I heard tell of. Marry, I must take this matter in hand and do what thou couldst not do, Sheriff, to wit, clear the forest of him and his band."

That night the King sat in the place that was set
apart for his lodging whilst in Nottingham Town.
With him were young Sir Henry of the Lea and two
other knights and three barons of Nottinghamshire;
but the King's mind still dwelt upon Robin Hood.
"Now," quoth he, "I would freely give a hundred
pounds to meet this roguish fellow, Robin Hood, and
to see somewhat of his doings in Sherwood Forest."

Then up spake Sir Hubert of Bingham, laughing:
"If your majesty hath such a desire upon you it is not
so hard to satisfy. If your majesty is willing to lose one
hundred pounds, I will engage to cause you not only to
meet this fellow, but to feast with him in Sherwood."

"Marry, Sir Hubert," quoth the King, "this
pleaseth me well. But how wilt thou cause me to meet
Robin Hood?"

"Why, thus," said Sir Hubert; "let your majesty
and us here present put on the robes of seven of the
Order of Black Friars, and let your majesty hang a
purse of one hundred pounds beneath your gown; then
let us undertake to ride from here to Mansfield Town

to-morrow, and, without I am much mistaken, we
will both meet with Robin Hood and dine with him
before the day be passed.''

"I like thy plan, Sir Hubert," quoth the King
merrily, "and to-morrow we will try it and see
whether there be virtue in it.''

So seven habits such as black friars wear were
brought, and the King and those about him having clad
themselves therein, and his majesty having hung a
purse with a hundred golden pounds in it beneath his
robes, they all went forth and mounted the mules that
had been brought to the door for them. Then the King
bade the Sheriff be silent as to their doings, and so they
set forth upon their way.

Onward they travelled, laughing and jesting, until
they passed through the open country; between bare
harvest fields whence the harvest had been gathered
home; through scattered glades that began to thicken
as they went farther along, till they came within the
heavy shade of the forest itself. They travelled in the
forest for several miles without meeting any one such

as they sought, until they had come to that part of the road that lay nearest to Newstead Abbey.

"By the holy Saint Martin," quoth the King, "I would that I had a better head for remembering things of great need. Here have we come away and brought never so much as a drop of anything to drink with us. Now I would give half a hundred pounds for somewhat to quench my thirst withal."

No sooner had the King so spoken, than out from the covert at the roadside stepped a tall fellow with yellow beard and hair and a pair of merry blue eyes. "Truly, holy brother," said he, laying his hand upon the King's bridle rein, "it were an unchristian thing not to give fitting answer to so fair a bargain. We keep an inn hereabouts, and for fifty pounds we will not only give thee wherewithal to quench thy thirst, but will set thee as noble a feast as ever thou didst tickle thy gullet withal." So saying he put his fingers to his lips and blew a shrill whistle. Then straightway the bushes and branches on either side of the road swayed and crackled and threescore broad-shouldered yeomen in Lincoln green burst out of the covert.

"How now, fellow," quoth the King, "who art thou, thou naughty rogue? Hast thou no regard for such holy men as we are?"

"Not a whit," quoth merry Robin Hood, for the fellow was he; "for in sooth all the holiness belonging to rich friars, such as ye are, one could drop into a thimble and the good wife would never feel it with the tip of her finger. As for my name, it is Robin Hood, and thou mayst have heard it before."

"Now out upon thee!" quoth King Richard. "Thou art a bold and naughty fellow and a lawless one withal, as I have often heard tell. Now, prythee, let me, and these brethren of mine, travel forward in peace and quietness."

"It may not be," said Robin, "for it would look but ill of us to let such goodly men travel onward with empty stomachs. But I doubt not that thou hast a fat purse to pay thy score at our inn since thou offerest freely so much wherewith to quench thy thirst. Show me thy purse, reverend brother, or I may perchance have to strip thy robes from thee to search for it myself"

"Nay, use no force," said the King sternly. "Here is my purse, but lay not thy lawless hands upon our person."

"Hut, tut," quoth merry Robin, "what proud words are these? Art thou the King of England, to talk so to me? Here, Will, take this purse and see what there is within."

Will Scarlet took the purse and counted out the money. Then Robin bade him keep fifty pounds for themselves, and put fifty back into the purse. This he handed to the King. "Here, brother," quoth he, "take this half of thy money, and thank Saint Martin, on whom thou didst call before, that thou hast fallen into the hands of such gentle rogues that they will not strip thee bare, as they might do. But wilt thou not put back thy cowl? for I would fain see thy face."

"Nay," said the King, drawing back, "I may not put back my cowl, for we seven have vowed that we will not show our faces for four and twenty hours."

"Then keep them covered in peace," said Robin, "and far be it from me to make you break your vows."

So he called seven of his yeomen and bade them
each one take a mule by the bridle; then, turning their
faces toward the depths of the woodlands, they journeyed onward until they came to the open glade and
the greenwood tree.

Little John, with threescore yeomen at his heels,
had also gone forth that morning to wait along the
roads and bring a rich guest to Sherwood glade, if such
might be his luck, for many with fat purses must travel
the roads at this time, when such great doings were
going on in Nottinghamshire; but though Little John
and so many others were gone, Friar Tuck and two-
score or more stout yeomen were seated or lying
around beneath the great tree, and when Robin and the
others came they leaped to their feet to meet him.

"By my soul," quoth merry King Richard, when
he had gotten down from his mule and stood looking
about him, "thou hast in very truth a fine lot of young
men about thee, Robin. Methinks King Richard himself would be glad of such a body-guard."

"These are not all of my fellows," said Robin,

proudly, "for threescore more of them are away on
business with my good right-hand man, Little John.
But, as for King Richard, I tell thee, brother, there is
not a man of us all but would pour out our blood like
water for him. Ye churchmen cannot rightly under-
stand our King; but we yeomen love him right loyally
for the sake of his brave doings which are so like our
own."

Presently a great crock was brought, from which
refreshment was poured for all the guests and for Robin
Hood. Then Robin held his cup aloft. "Stay!" cried
he. "Tarry till I give you a pledge. Here is to good
King Richard of great renown, and may all enemies to
him be confounded."

At this the King laughed. "Then," quoth he,
"good fellow, we have paid well for our fare, so canst
thou not show us some merry entertainment? I have
oft heard that ye are wondrous archers; wilt thou not
show us somewhat of your skill?"

"With all my heart," said Robin; "we are always
pleased to show our guests all the sport that is to

be seen. Ho, lads! set up a garland at the end of the glade.''

Then the yeomen ran to do their master's bidding. The mark at which they were to shoot was set up at sixscore paces distance. It was a garland of leaves and flowers two spans in width, which same was hung upon a stake in front of a broad tree-trunk. ''There,'' quoth Robin, ''yon is a fair mark, lads. Each of you shoot three arrows thereat; and if any fellow misseth by so much as one arrow, he shall have a buffet of Will Scarlet's fist.''

''Hearken to him!'' quoth Friar Tuck. ''Why, master, thou dost bestow buffets from thy strapping nephew as though they were love taps from some bouncing lass. I warrant thou art safe to hit the garland thyself, or thou wouldst not be so free of his cuffing.''

First David of Doncaster shot, and lodged all three of his arrows within the garland. ''Well done, David!'' cried Robin, ''thou hast saved thine ears from a warming this day.'' Next Midge, the Miller, shot, and he, also, lodged his arrows in the garland. Then followed Wat, the Tinker, but alas for him! for one of his shafts missed the mark by the breadth of two fingers.

"Come hither, fellow," said Will Scarlet, in his soft, gentle voice; "I owe thee somewhat that I would pay forthwith." Then Wat, the Tinker, came forward and stood in front of Will Scarlet, screwing up his face and shutting his eyes tightly, as though he already felt his ears ringing with the buffet. Will Scarlet rolled up his sleeve, and, standing on tiptoe to give the greater swing to his arm, he struck with might and main. "*Whoof!*" came his palm against the Tinker's head, and down went stout Wat to the grass, heels over head, as the wooden image at the fair goes down when the skillful player throws a cudgel at it. Then, as the Tinker sat up upon the grass, rubbing his ear and winking and blinking at the bright stars that danced before his eyes, the yeomen roared with mirth till the forest rang. As for King Richard, he laughed till the tears ran down his cheeks. Thus the band shot, each in turn, some getting off scot free, and some winning a buffet that always sent them to the grass. And now, last of

all, Robin took his place, and all was hushed as he shot.
The first shaft he shot split a piece from the stake on
which the garland was hung; the second shaft lodged
within an inch of the other. "By my halidom," said
King Richard to himself, "I would give a thousand
pounds for this fellow to be one of my guard!" And
now, for the third time Robin shot; but, alas for him!
the arrow was ill-feathered, and, wavering to one side,
it smote an inch outside the garland.

At this a great roar went up, those of the yeomen
who sat upon the grass rolling over and over and
shouting with laughter, for never before had they seen
their master so miss his mark; but Robin flung his
bow upon the ground with vexation. "Now, out upon
it!" cried he. "That shaft had an ill feather to it, for
I felt it as it left my fingers. Give me a clean arrow,
and I will engage to split the wand with it."

At these words the yeomen laughed louder than
ever. "Nay, good uncle," said Will Scarlet, in his soft,
sweet voice, "thou hast had thy fair chance and hast
missed thine aim out and out. I swear the arrow was as

good as any that hath been loosed this day. Come hither; I owe thee somewhat, and would fain pay it.''

''Go, good master,'' roared Friar Tuck, ''and may my blessing go with thee. Thou hast bestowed these love-taps of Will Scarlet's with great freedom. It were a pity an thou gottest not thine own share.''

''It may not be,'' said merry Robin. ''I am king here, and no subject may raise hand against the king. But even our great King Richard may yield to the holy Pope without shame, and even take a tap from him by way of penance; therefore I will yield myself to this holy friar, who seemeth to be one in authority, and will take my punishment from him.'' Thus saying, he turned to the King, ''I prythee, brother, wilt thou take my punishing into thy holy hands?''

''With all my heart,'' quoth merry King Richard, rising from where he was sitting. ''I owe thee somewhat for having lifted a heavy weight of fifty pounds from my purse. So make room for him on the green, lads.''

''An thou makest me tumble,'' quoth Robin, ''I

will freely give thee back thy fifty pounds; but I tell
thee, brother, if thou makest me not feel grass all
along my back, I will take away every farthing thou
hast for thy boastful speech."

"So be it," said the King, "I am willing to ven-
ture it." Thereupon he rolled up his sleeve and
showed an arm that made the yeomen stare. But
Robin, with his feet wide apart, stood firmly planted,
waiting the other, smiling. Then the King swung back
his arm, and, balancing himself a moment, he delivered
a buffet at Robin that fell like a thunderbolt. Down
went Robin headlong upon the grass, for the stroke
would have felled a stone wall. Then how the yeomen
shouted with laughter till their sides ached, for never
had they seen such a buffet given in all their lives. As
for Robin, he presently sat up and looked all around
him, as though he had dropped from a cloud and had
lit in a place he had never seen before. After a while,
still gazing about him at his laughing yeomen, he put
his finger-tips softly to his ear and felt all around it
tenderly. "Will Scarlet," said he, "count this fellow

out his fifty pounds; I want nothing more either of his money or of him. A murrain seize him and his buffeting! I would that I had taken my dues from thee, for I verily believe he hath deafened mine ears from ever hearing again.''

Then, while gusts of laughter still broke from the band, Will Scarlet counted out the fifty pounds, and the King dropped it back into his purse again. ''I give thee thanks, fellow,'' said he, ''and if ever thou shouldst wish for another box of the ear to match the one thou hast, come to me and I will fit thee with it for naught.''

So spake the merry King; but, even as he ended, there came suddenly the sound of many voices, and out from the covert burst Little John and threescore men. Across the glade they came running, and, as they came, Little John shouted to Robin: ''Make haste, good master, to escape! King Richard left Nottingham Town this very morning, and cometh to seek thee in the woodlands. I know not how he cometh, for it was but a rumor of this that reached me; nevertheless, I

Merry·Robin· hath·the· worst·of· a· Bargain·

know that it is the truth. But tell me, good master, who are these who are with us to-day?''

''Why,'' quoth merry Robin, rising from the grass, ''these are certain gentle guests that came with us from the high-road over by Newstead Abbey. I know not their names, but I have become right well acquaint with this lusty fellow's palm this morning. Marry, the pleasure of this acquaintance hath cost me a deaf ear and fifty pounds to boot!''

But Little John looked keenly at the tall friar, who, drawing himself up to his full height, looked fixedly back at the yeoman. Then of a sudden Little John grew pale, for he knew who it was that he looked upon. ''The King!'' he cried, ''The King!'' and quickly he flung himself upon his knees before the other. At this, the King, seeing that Little John knew him, threw back his cowl, and all the yeomen saw his face and knew him also. Down they fell upon their knees, nor could they say a word. Then the King looked all around right grimly, and, last of all, his glance came back and rested again upon Robin Hood.

Then at last his face broke into a smile. "Why,
how now, good Robin," quoth he, "methinks we owe
thee somewhat for so round a buffet. Rise all of you,
for ye shall suffer no harm through me this day, for it
were pity that a merry time should end in such a
manner as to mar its joyousness."

Then all arose and the King beckoned Robin
Hood to come to him. "How now," quoth he, "is
thine ear still too deaf to hear me speak?"

"Mine ears would be deafened in death ere they
would cease to hear your majesty's voice," said Robin.
"As for the blow that your majesty struck me, I would
say that though my sins are haply many, methinks they
have been paid up in full thereby."

"Thinkest thou so?" said the King with somewhat of sternness in his voice. "Now I tell thee that
but for three things, to wit, my mercifulness, my love
for a stout woodsman, and the loyalty thou hast
avowed for me, thine ears, mayhap, might have been
more tightly closed than ever a buffet from me could
have shut them. Talk not lightly of thy sins, good

Robin. But come, look up. Thy danger is past, for hereby I give thee and all thy band free pardon. But, in sooth, I cannot let you roam the forest as ye have done in the past; therefore I will take thee at thy word, when thou didst say thou wouldst give thy service to me, and thou shalt go back to London with me. We will take that bold knave Little John also, and likewise thy cousin, Will Scarlet, and thy minstrel, Allan a Dale. As for the rest of thy band, we will take their names and have them duly recorded as royal rangers; for methinks it were wiser to have them changed to law-abiding caretakers of our deer in Sherwood than to leave them run at large as outlawed slayers thereof. But now get a feast ready, for I would fain see how ye live here in the leafy woodlands.''

The next day the King took leave of Nottingham Town; so Robin Hood and Little John and Will Scarlet and Allan a Dale shook hands with all the rest of the band, kissing the cheeks of each man, and swearing that they would often come to Sherwood and

see them. Then each mounted his horse and rode away
in the train of the King.

Thus end the merry adventures of Robin Hood;
for, in spite of his promise, it was many a year ere he
saw Sherwood again. After a year of two at court Little
John came back to Nottinghamshire, where he lived
in an orderly way, though within sight of Sherwood,
and where he achieved great fame as the champion of
all England with the quarterstaff. Will Scarlet after a
time came back to his own home, whence he had been
driven by his unlucky killing of his father's steward.
The rest of the band did their duty as royal rangers
right well. But Robin Hood and Allan a Dale did not
come again to Sherwood so quickly, for thus it was:—

Robin, through his great fame as an archer, became
a favorite with the King, so that he speedily arose
in rank to be the chief of all the yeomen. At last the
King, seeing how faithful and how loyal he was,
created him Earl of Huntingdon; so Robin followed
the King to the wars, and found his time so full that he
had no chance to come back to Sherwood for even

so much as a day. As for Allan a Dale, he followed Robin Hood and shared in all his ups and downs of life.

Thus all things have an end, but not such a lucky ending as befell Robin Hood and his band of stout yeomen in famous Sherwood Forest.

THE END.